W9-CEI-349

KEEPER OF THE STARS

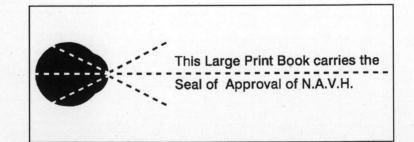

This Large Print Book carries the
Seal of Approval of N.A.V.H.

A KINGS MEADOW ROMANCE

KEEPER OF THE STARS

ROBIN LEE HATCHER

THORNDIKE PRESS

A part of Gale, Cengage Learning

GALE
CENGAGE Learning®

Farmington Hills, Mich • San Francisco • New York • Waterville, Maine
Meriden, Conn • Mason, Ohio • Chicago

GALE
CENGAGE Learning

LIBRARY OF CONGRESS CATALOGING-IN-PUBLICATION DATA

Names: Hatcher, Robin Lee, author.
Title: Keeper of the stars : a Kings Meadow novel / Robin Lee Hatcher.
Description: Large print edition. | Waterville, Maine : Thorndike Press Large Print,
    2016. | © 2016 | Series: A Kings Meadow novel ; 3 | Series: Thorndike Press large
    print Christian fiction
Identifiers: LCCN 2015044741 | ISBN 9781410486721 (hardback) | ISBN 1410486729
    (hardcover)
Subjects: LCSH: Large type books. | BISAC: FICTION / Christian / General. | GSAFD:
    Love stories. | Christian fiction.
Classification: LCC PS3558.A73574 K44 2016b | DDC 813/.54—dc23
LC record available at http://lccn.loc.gov/2015044741

Published in 2016 by arrangement with Thomas Nelson, Inc., a division
of HarperCollins Christian Publishing, Inc.

Printed in Mexico
2 3 4 5 6 7 20 19 18 17 16

To the Keeper of the stars

PROLOGUE

SEPTEMBER 30

An unusually cold wind cut through the Kings Meadow Cemetery on the day they laid Penny's brother, Bradley Evan Cartwright, to rest. It felt as if it cut through her heart as well, slicing her in two. She would never again see her little brother's sweet smile. She would never again hear him laugh. She would never again have to be on the alert for one of his practical jokes.

And I'll never get to tell him I'm sorry for the things I said in anger.

Seated beside her in the front row of mourners, her dad put his arm around her shoulders and drew her close to his side. It was meant to be a comforting gesture, but it was pointless for him to try. She couldn't be comforted. Not in this.

Reverend Tom Butler ended his graveside prayer with a soft "Amen." Then he walked over to Penny and her dad, his face schooled into a sympathetic expression, his eyes filled

7

with kindness. "I am so very sorry, Rodney," he said as he took hold of her dad's right hand between both of his own.

Her dad nodded in silence.

Tom repeated his words of condolence to Penny. Like her father, she nodded, her throat too tight to squeeze out a reply.

Chet Leonard, his wife, and his sons were next. Leaning down, Chet said, "If I can do anything . . . If you ever need to talk or just be with someone who understands what it means to lose a son . . ." He let his voice trail into silence.

Charlie Regal, Brad's best friend since first grade, came close, looked about to speak, and then shook his head as he turned to walk away.

More people came forward. A few shed tears as they whispered words that Penny no longer heard.

Twelve years ago, pneumonia had taken Penny's mom at the age of forty-five. Despite how ill her mom had been, sixteen-year-old Penny hadn't believed she would die. Perhaps pneumonia still took the lives of those who were frail, like the elderly or little children. But someone in the best of health like her mom had been? How could that happen with all the advances in modern medicine? Charlotte Cartwright's death had rocked the family.

And now Brad . . . Brad, who hadn't even reached his twenty-third birthday. He'd finished college at the end of last year, a full semester ahead of schedule. He could have had a brilliant future before him for the taking. But he hadn't even bothered to attend his own graduation ceremony. He'd come home for Christmas and, soon after, packed up and headed for Nashville, exchanging an engineering career for a stupid set of drums and a life on the road as part of a band.

And now he's dead.

She shivered. Not from the cold but from the emotions that roiled inside of her. Anger. Exasperation. Frustration.

Stupid. Stupid. Stupid.

The last of the mourners finally walked toward their cars. The reverend stood at a respectful distance, as if waiting to see if he would be needed.

"Let's go home, Pen," her dad said, his voice breaking at the end.

"Okay."

They rose in unison and turned from the flower-covered coffin. It wasn't a long ways to her dad's truck. They moved slowly, arms entwined, watching the uneven ground before them. They were almost to the truck when someone stepped into their path.

9

The first thing Penny saw were the toes of a fancy pair of cowboy boots poking out from beneath trousers with a fine crease. She looked up, expecting to see a familiar face, expecting to hear more words of solace. But it wasn't a lifelong friend or neighbor, and when she saw who it was, her breath caught. It couldn't be him. It couldn't be that man. Not here. Not here in Kings Meadow.

"Mr. Cartwright," he said to her dad as he removed a black Stetson from his head. "I'm Trevor Reynolds. I . . . I'm sorry about Brad. He was a good kid."

If her dad was surprised by Trevor's appearance at his son's funeral, it didn't show in his voice. "Thank you."

Trevor's gaze slid to her. "You must be Penny. I —"

She slapped him. Hard.

His eyes widened. His mouth thinned. But he didn't move, didn't make a sound.

"You don't belong here," she said with icy resolve.

For a second Trevor looked as if he might protest, but instead he took a wide step off to the side and allowed father and daughter to pass.

Her dad waited until they arrived at the passenger door of his truck before he said,

10

"You shouldn't have done that, Pen."

She disagreed. She should have done it. She'd wanted to do even more. She'd wanted to haul back and slam Trevor Reynolds as hard as she could with a tight fist. He was the reason her brother was dead, and he deserved to bleed, to feel pain, to —

"Hate and blame won't bring Brad back," her dad added.

Somehow she held back the tears that burned her throat and eyes. If she started to cry, she feared she would never stop. Tears would mean she was weak, and she had to stay strong. For her dad. For herself.

For Brad.

BRAD

2003

On the day his mom died, Brad climbed his favorite tree and didn't plan on ever coming down. Maybe he would have stayed forever if Penny hadn't come looking for him. She climbed good . . . for a girl.

"You need to come inside, Brad," she said as she settled on a sturdy branch. "Dad's ready to put dinner on the table."

He sniffed, then wiped his tears with his forearm. "I'm not hungry."

"You've gotta come in anyhow."

He stared down at his hands, now resting on his thighs, folded into tight fists. He didn't want to go inside. Every room in the house was filled with memories of his mom, and it hurt too much to think about her.

"Please, buddy."

He heard his tears mirrored in her voice.

"We've gotta stick together now, Brad. We need each other."

"Okay," he whispered at last. "I'll come down."

She looked at him in silence before standing on the branch. Only when her feet touched the ground a short while later did Brad begin his promised descent. Once he was down, Penny put an arm around his shoulders and gave him a quick squeeze.

"It's gonna be all right," she whispered.

He might be just a kid, but he knew his big sister didn't believe that any more than he did. It wasn't going to be all right. Their mom wasn't ever coming home again. She wasn't ever going to go camping with them in the mountains or go riding horseback with them along the river or bake him another birthday cake. She wouldn't ever again cheer for him at a soccer game on the school field or shout with joy when he made it up on water skis during one of their trips up to McCall. He wouldn't ever again see her get all mushy with Dad, the way she'd liked to do in the evening when they were all watching a movie.

Brad and Penny walked toward the front of the house, and when they rounded the corner, he saw that only his dad's truck was parked in the barnyard now. Friends of his parents had been coming by all afternoon, almost the instant word about his mom had gotten out. Some had brought flowers. Some had brought food. Some had just come to say they were sorry. Now, as twilight settled over the valley, the friends were all gone. Gone back to their families and their homes.

Brad had to make himself go inside the house. It felt empty. Haunted almost.

"Dad," Penny called out. "We're back." She kept her arm around Brad's shoulders, urging him toward the kitchen with a gentle pressure.

It was a sad dinner, the only sounds the clicking of knives and forks against plates. Brad didn't taste a bite. Whatever he swallowed might as well have been sawdust.

Maybe nothing would ever taste good again.

CHAPTER 1
NOVEMBER 30

Trevor Reynolds glanced around the studio apartment, located three blocks from the main drag in Kings Meadow. At one time it had been a detached garage, and the owner hadn't tried to disguise its original purpose from the outside. Inside, the furnishings were simple and spare, but good enough to suit Trevor's purposes for however long he was here. He'd stayed in far worse places in his early years on the road.

"I'll take it," he told the landlord, Harry Adams, a thin, white-haired man with stooped shoulders, a shuffling step, and a ready smile.

"Well, that's great. Great. Are you in town for long, Mr. Reynolds?"

Trevor slipped his wallet from his back pocket. "I'm not sure." He pulled out several bills. "First and last month's rent. Right?"

"Indeed it is." In exchange for the money,

17

the landlord handed him the key to the door.

Trevor walked to the small refrigerator and opened it. The light went on at the back, showing a pristine interior.

"Grocery store's just a few blocks away," Mr. Adams said. "Open until nine."

"What about restaurants?" He closed the refrigerator door and turned toward the landlord again.

The old man chuckled. "Only got two. Got a drive-through a couple blocks over from the Merc. Good burgers and fries. Then there's the Tamarack Grill that you passed on your way into town. That's your sit-down choice. Nice menu, especially since they hired that Nichols fella."

Trevor remembered seeing the Tamarack Grill. That's where he would go now. He'd had his fill of fast food while traveling the two thousand miles from Nashville to Kings Meadow. According to the map app on his phone, winter driving conditions had made the trip take three days longer than it should have. And not knowing how many miles he'd be able to travel each day had also made it impossible to book motel reservations in advance. That hadn't mattered as long as he'd been traveling the freeway. Any

18

motel in any town, big or small, had sufficed.

But he should have known things would be different up here in these mountains. Kings Meadow didn't have a motel, and the bed-and-breakfast he'd stopped at earlier wouldn't have any available rooms until tomorrow. It was a good thing he'd grabbed a local newspaper when he stopped for gas as he rolled into town. The paper was where he'd seen the advertisement for this apartment. The rent was fair — cheap, actually — and he didn't need anything fancy.

A yawn overtook him, a reminder that he'd been on the road since four o'clock that morning. A moment later his stomach growled. He'd pushed himself hard, determined to reach Kings Meadow while it was still daylight. He hadn't eaten a meal since breakfast. That had been somewhere in Utah. All he wanted now was a decent meal and a good night's sleep. Tomorrow would be soon enough to stock the cupboards, get settled into his new living quarters, and figure out what he was supposed to do next.

"Well," the landlord said, intruding on Trevor's thoughts, "you give a holler if you need anything. And you're always welcome to use my phone if you need it."

"I've got one." He patted his pocket.

"If you mean a cell phone, those gadgets don't work much in these parts. Mountains too high and too close, and no company's bothered to bring in one of them tower thingies. If you want to talk to folks, you're gonna have to get yourself a regular phone. Landlines, I think they call 'em."

Trevor remembered now. The day of the funeral, he'd tried to use his mobile phone. There hadn't been any reception. Not until he'd gotten close to Boise again had service resumed. But he'd figured it was a temporary problem. Hadn't considered it was an ongoing issue. He'd known he was coming to a small town. He hadn't figured on it being so backward it wouldn't have cell phone service.

Just as well. You don't need to hear from anybody who'd know your number anyway.

"Thanks, Mr. Adams. You've been a big help."

If the landlord felt as if he'd been dismissed — which he had — he didn't show it. Just smiled again and told Trevor to enjoy his dinner. Then he shuffled out of the studio apartment and along the snowy pathway to the main house.

Hunching his shoulders against the cold, Trevor hurried out to his truck and grabbed his duffel bag and guitar case from the backseat. Several more trips emptied the pickup bed of the tarp-covered boxes holding the remainder of his possessions. At least the possessions he'd considered important enough to bring with him. More boxes and all of his furniture were in a storage unit in Nashville. When he went back to Tennessee, he'd be glad for them.

With hunger becoming a more demanding sensation in his gut, he left the collection of belongings in the center of the room, grabbed his truck keys, and headed out the door. He drove the three blocks to Main Street, then followed it west until the restaurant's sign came into view. The parking lot on the side of the building had six or seven cars in it. That was probably a rush of customers for Kings Meadow.

He pulled into the first open space and got out, glad he wouldn't have to walk far in the bitter wind. Even gladder that he wouldn't have to sleep in his truck — which had seemed a real possibility — even for just one night.

The warm interior of the Tamarack Grill was a welcome relief. He stopped next to the sign that told him to wait to be seated. He didn't have to stand there long. A young woman, carrying laminated menus in the crook of her left arm, came toward him, a smile on her lips. Her gaze slowly traveled the length of him before meeting his eyes again.

"Welcome to the Tamarack Grill. Just one tonight?"

"Just one."

Her smile broadened.

Not to be vain, but he knew that look.

"Right this way." She led him to a table close to an open fireplace made of stones.

Trevor removed his Stetson and put it on the seat of one chair, then sat on the other, his right shoulder toward the fire.

"May I bring you something to drink?" the waitress asked as she set a menu on the table before him.

"Diet Coke, with lemon."

"I'll be right back." Still smiling, she departed.

Trevor's gaze took in the other tables in the room. Two families with young kids. A middle-aged woman eating by herself. Several couples of various ages. Off to the far right was the bar area. Three men sat on stools, sipping beverages and watching news on a television up high on the wall. Until a couple of months ago, that's where Trevor would have started a meal. Sitting at the bar, knocking back a Jack and Coke.

No more. The night of the accident, he'd

had a wake-up call. He'd been living reck-lessly for years, in all kinds of ways. He could have easily died that night, but he'd been given a second chance. Brad Cart-wright hadn't been that lucky.

A raw ache burned in his chest whenever he thought about Brad. Logically, Trevor knew the accident hadn't been his fault. He'd been asleep in the backseat. Brad had been at the wheel. But all the same, it felt like his fault.

And I'm not the only one who feels it's my fault.

In his mind — for what seemed the thou-sandth time — he saw the fury in Penny Cartwright's eyes at the moment she'd slapped him on the day of the funeral. He touched his cheek, as if he could still feel the sting of the blow.

The waitress returned with his drink. "Are you ready to order?"

He hadn't looked at the menu yet, but a quick glance found something that would do. He pointed to it, chose the two sides that came with the meal, then handed her the menu. "Thanks."

She gave him another of her ready smiles before walking away, and for a split second he considered asking her what time her shift ended. But no. Pretty girls weren't why he'd come to Kings Meadow. He was here to keep a promise to a dying friend — and hopefully straighten out his life in the process.

Penny turned the dead bolt in the entrance door of the library. Then she leaned her forehead against the cold glass, closing her eyes and drawing a deep breath. Some days it felt as if she had to force herself to breathe, force herself to go on living.

Stop it! Stop it now!

Stiffening her spine, she turned away from the door and walked to the office behind the checkout counter, where she retrieved her purse from the bottom drawer of her desk. A glance at the clock on the wall told her she was running late. Dad would have dinner waiting for her.

Maybe I shouldn't have returned to work this soon.

Perhaps not. But she had no choice. Not really. She'd used up all of her paid time off — both bereavement and vacation time — and she and Dad needed her paycheck. Their finances had already been stretched thin by the staggering cost of an unexpected funeral —

No. Stop. Don't think about it.

Lifting her head and straightening her

shoulders, she left the office, turning off the light as she passed through the doorway. She went to the back door of the library, where she switched off all but the security lights that softly illumined the building whenever the library was closed. Then she went outside, locking the door behind her.

Blowing snow stung Penny's cheeks as she hurried to her parked car. She started the engine to let it warm — wouldn't it be wonderful to have one of those cars that started with a press of a button on a key fob? — then grabbed the scraper so she could clean the snow and frost off her windshield. Trying not to let her teeth chatter, she worked as fast as possible, making a complete circle around the vehicle. At last she slipped behind the wheel with a breathy, "Ooooh."

The drive to the Cartwright ranch took about twenty minutes on the snow-packed roads. It wasn't a big spread — not like the Leonard operation at the north end of the valley — but it was big enough to fulfill her dad's boyhood dream of being a cattle rancher. Most years he turned a small profit from the sale of his calves. He earned the rest of his income from the work he did as a carpenter. Good enough in the summer. Scarce in the winter months. And these

25

days, due to some health issues, he struggled with his daily chores.

Penny's return to Kings Meadow after getting her master's degree was supposed to have been temporary. Only until Brad graduated from college. Her brother could have worked as an engineer in Boise with an easy commute to and from the ranch. Their dad would have had the help he needed, and Brad would have had a career he could have grown in. That had been the plan. But since when did life go as planned? *Temporary* had become four years, and here she was, living at home at the age of twenty-eight. The best thing to come out of her return to Kings Meadow was her job as the director of the district library. Anywhere else, she wouldn't have had a prayer of such a position. Too young, they would have said. Too little experience. They would have been right on both counts. But this was Kings Meadow, where she was known, where her father was known. And besides, there hadn't been an abundance of applicants for the position.

She should be thankful for it. She *was* thankful for it. If only she didn't feel so unhappy, reminded at every turn of the loved ones who were gone forever. If only . . .

Lights from the house twinkled at her in the darkness. She slowed the car as she approached the driveway. The tires slid a little, but with four-wheel drive she was able to pull out of the slide and make the turn safely. The hard-packed snow beneath the tires bumped her around until she reached the concrete floor of the garage. Fresh snow fell in earnest as she hurried toward the front door.

Inside the house, she called, "Dad, I'm home."

He poked his head out of the kitchen. "Good timing. Food's ready to go on the table."

"Give me a second to change and wash up, and I'll be right there."

"Is it still snowing?"

Halfway up the stairs, she answered, "Yes. Looks like the storm will last awhile."

In her room, Penny changed out of her work clothes and into a comfortable pair of jeans and a sky-blue cable-knit sweater. Her shoes she replaced with sheepskin-lined slippers, appropriate for the winter weather. Then she went into the bathroom, where she freed her hair from the clasp that kept it away from her face while at work, followed by a quick wash of her hands.

When she entered the dining room a few

27

minutes later, her dad was setting a casserole dish in the center of the table. Shepherd's pie. Again. It was her father's go-to recipe when he couldn't think of anything else to make. She rounded the table and gave him a kiss on the cheek. "Thanks for cooking dinner on the nights I work late."

"I'm glad to do it, Pen. You shouldn't have to work all day and then come home to cook supper when all I'd be doing is sitting around, waiting for you."

She wanted to ask if his back was better today, but he despised the question. Her dad still did a lot of work around the place, even when the pain was bad.

If only her brother had come home . . .

"Let's eat," her dad said.

Penny took her usual spot at the table and averted her eyes from the two empty chairs. She tried to look only at the serving dishes and at her father. Anywhere else was rife with emotional danger.

Her dad said the blessing before sliding the casserole dish closer to her. "Careful. It's hot."

She stuck the serving spoon into the meat-and-vegetable dish and scooped out a small serving.

"You need to eat more than that, Penny."

"This is plenty, Dad. Honest."

"Not enough to keep a bird alive."

Missing tugged at Penny's heart. How often had her mom said those very same words to her?

"How was it to be back at the library?"

"Okay." She shrugged. "How was your day?"

"Okay," he answered with the smallest of smiles.

What a pair of liars we are.

Penny brought a bite of the casserole to her mouth, blew on it, and then ate it. Her taste buds tried to tell her the food had flavor, but it still seemed bland on her tongue. Somehow she managed to swallow and take the next bite.

"It'll get better, Pen."

She kept her gaze on her plate. "It's good."

"I wasn't talking about the food."

Tears welled. *I know,* she mouthed, looking up at last.

She'd learned that going through the grief process took as long as it took. Not one day more or one day less. And it was different for each person. There were no quick fixes, no magic words to make the pain of missing go away any faster.

The difference this time — between when she'd lost her mom and when she'd lost her brother — was the anger. Tears weren't enough for her. Grief wasn't enough. A broken heart wasn't enough. Bitter anger had formed a knot in her gut — a knot that showed no signs of easing. She was angry with Brad for being so foolish, for not returning to Kings Meadow when he was supposed to. Angry with Trevor Reynolds for enticing Brad to live a life on the road, for making her brother forget that he was the kind of person who kept his promises. And, if she was honest, angry with God for taking away another member of her family.

Some days it felt as if the anger would eat her up from the inside out.

Some days she wished it would.

That night, while seated in the large, over-stuffed chair in the corner of his bedroom, Rodney closed his eyes. Before his wife passed away, the couple had been in the habit of praying together in this same corner before retiring. There had been two chairs back then. Now there was need for only one, and even after a dozen years he missed the feel of Charlotte's hand in his as they prayed at the end of a day.

He drew in a long breath and released it slowly. "How do I help her, Lord?"

Even before Brad's death Rodney had been concerned for his daughter. Penny seemed to have forgotten how to enjoy life. She worried over him. She worried over money. She worried over what tomorrow would bring. And now she was angry too. She tried not to let him see it, but she never succeeded.

"What happened to my bright, shiny Penny?" he whispered.

In his mind he saw the laughing, happy, confident child she had been. Riding beside him in the truck, chattering away about what had happened that day at school. Showing her little brother how to skip rocks across the surface of the river. Camping in the mountains with the family. She'd been fearless back then, perhaps because she'd had such trust in God. That trust seemed to have been snuffed out on the night her brother died.

His heart ached at the thought. For as long as he lived he would miss his son, the same way he continued to miss his wife. But there was comfort in knowing Brad had loved the Lord and was with Him now.

" 'But we do not want you to be uninformed, brethren,' " he quoted aloud, " 'about those who are asleep, so that you will not grieve as do the rest who have no hope.' "

Penny needs hope, Lord. She needs Your hope. Show me how to help her find it.

CHAPTER 2

Judging by the snow on Trevor's truck, a good eight to ten inches of the white stuff had fallen overnight. But this morning the sky was a cloudless blue, and the reflection off the snow almost blinded him before he put on his sunglasses. A California boy, born and raised, Trevor appreciated the beauty of the frosty wonderland all around him, but he wasn't fond of the cold that came with it, or the slick roads. And from the look of things, he could be in for a very long winter with plenty of all three.

If I'm here that long.

He shook off the thought. He wouldn't be of much use to himself or anyone else if he started wondering when he'd get out of here. He'd made a hasty promise to Brad Cartwright. He wasn't sure he'd meant to keep it. In fact, after his disastrous first trip to Kings Meadow for the funeral, he'd tried to forget ever making the promise to come to Idaho, to spend time with Brad's family. Brad hadn't actually said he needed Trevor to help his family, but with all the things the guy had shared, he figured that was the reason. And since he didn't know how to help, why keep the promise? But again and again over the past weeks, he'd imagined himself on the side of the road, holding Brad, telling him he'd be okay. And every time he'd imagined it, he'd remembered the promise. He couldn't shake free of it.

So here he was at last, a stranger in a hole-in-the-wall town, hoping to do something for two people he didn't know who would probably hate the sight of him.

A broom leaned against the wall inside the carport. Later he planned to ask his landlord if he could park in the empty space. For now, he grabbed the broom and went to work, sweeping the snow off the front windshield and hood of his truck. Next he got the scraper and made quick work of the frost that had formed on the glass.

The drive to the Merc on Main Street — the town's one and only grocery store — took no time at all. Judging by the empty parking lot, he was the only customer at this time on a weekday morning. Or maybe it was the fresh blanket of snow that had kept shoppers at home. He parked close to the entrance and went inside.

A woman behind a checkout stand greeted him with a friendly, "Good morning."

"Morning," he returned with a nod.

"You need any help finding something, you let me know."

It was obvious he'd been immediately pegged as a newcomer. He gave a second nod, grabbed a shopping cart, and started down the far right aisle.

The studio apartment he'd rented came with some basic household items — a few pots and pans; some plastic storage containers; table service, plates, bowls, and drinking glasses. Mr. Adams even provided one set of sheets, a couple of blankets, and a down comforter for the double bed, plus some cleaning supplies. Trevor was sure to discover more things he would need as time passed, but for now he would focus on food items. Mostly meals that were quick and easy to fix, since he wasn't of much use in the kitchen. Pasta and seasoning from a box, add hamburger and water, and simmer for fifteen to twenty minutes. That was good enough for him most days. Plus it was cheap, and since he had no idea when or if he would find work in this remote burg, or how long he would be here, he would need to be careful with the money he had in savings. Right now it was a tidy sum, but he'd learned that could change in a hurry.

Life as a musician had had its ups and downs. Trevor had known times of abundance and other times of near famine. Nashville had never come pounding on his door, although there were times he'd thought it was about to happen. But as the years had gone by, he'd been less hopeful that he would ever have the success he'd craved. Stardom had eluded him. Instead of fame, he and the guys in his band had played bars and county fairs and music festivals, one after another, week in and week out. So many that they all blended together in his memory.

"You could have made something of your life. You could've had a real career. What a waste." His father's words were like a blow to the side of his head. They hurt, even now. The passage of time hadn't helped at all.

Trevor gave his head a shake and tried to focus on what his next steps should be. Kings Meadow had at least one bar besides the one inside the Tamarack Grill. But Trevor doubted either place was looking for a singer and guitarist. Just as well. He needed to look for a different kind of employment while he was here. Although what that might be, he didn't have a clue. Like most musicians, he'd put in hours as a waiter, a janitor, even a carpenter. What was it they said? Jack of all trades and master of none. Only that wasn't quite true of him. He *was* a master with the guitar, and he had *exactly* the right kind of voice to make it as a country singer. He'd even written a few good songs, if only somebody in the business had been willing to give them a chance.

For the third time in less than an hour, he abruptly changed the direction his thoughts were headed. Going down that road, asking why, trying to figure out what he could have done differently, never got him anywhere. Never had. Never would.

His cart filled with a little of this and a little of that, Trevor pushed it to the check-out counter. The woman who had greeted him earlier began to run the items over the scanner and then bag them, the prices showing on a display to her right.

"You're new to Kings Meadow," she said after a few moments.

"Yes."

"You got family in town?" She glanced up, curiosity in her eyes.

"No. No family."

She passed five pounds of hamburger over

the scanner. "Looks like you mean to stay awhile."

This time he nodded, then shrugged. He might not have lived in Kings Meadow longer than a day, but he knew from Brad that it was tough to keep secrets in a small town. Trevor would just as soon keep his business to himself.

When the groceries were tallied up, he ran his credit card through the machine and signed the small screen. His receipt spit out of a slot on the register, and as the woman handed it to him, he asked, "Where would a guy go around here if he wanted to find work?"

Her eyes widened. "December's a hard time of year to find a job."

"I know."

"Lots of folks drive down to Boise every day."

Trevor didn't like the sound of that.

"Kings Meadow doesn't have an employment agency, but the mayor's office usually knows if somebody's looking to hire. You could try there." She pointed out the glass front of the store. "Take Main back thataway a few blocks. It'll be on your right. You can't miss it."

"Thanks." He put the last of the grocery bags into the cart. "You've been helpful."

He headed for the exit doors.

A place to stay. Food in the fridge. Hopefully some leads on employment. And then it would be time to see the Cartwrights.

With any luck, Penny Cartwright wouldn't slap him a second time.

Penny dropped hay into the manger, then paused long enough to watch the mare inside the stall begin to eat. Harmony was an eight-year-old buckskin quarter horse, pregnant with her first foal. Penny's dad had bought the mare as a graduation present the spring Penny received her bachelor's degree. Then, early this year, he had worked some sort of trade with Chet Leonard in exchange for breeding Harmony with one of the Leonard champion studs. Dad wouldn't tell her exactly what he'd traded since the stud service had been his birthday present to her. It was quite possible the foal would be worth more than anything else on her dad's ranch, if all went well. Not that she would want to sell it.

With a sigh, she turned away from the stall. She had a few more horses to feed and scratch to throw around for the hens before her chores would be done.

Meow.

She looked up. Tux — Penny called Brad's

black-and-white cat "fourteen-pounds-of-don't-touch-me" — paced the length of the loft, continuing to meow in that unfriendly way of hers.

"Your food's inside, you no-good cat." Then she muttered, "Not that you appreciate it."

Her brother had been the only human Tux ever liked. When Brad was around, the feline had loved to curl up in his lap or on his chest and purr so loudly the sound seemed to make the room vibrate. But if anybody else tried to pick her up, Tux would hiss and sometimes lash out with her claws.

Suddenly Penny would have liked nothing more than to hold that nasty-tempered cat and pretend Brad was still able to do the same.

Fred and Ginger, the border collies, began to bark outside the barn, and Tux went into hiding. If the dogs were in the barnyard, that meant her dad had already returned from feeding the cattle. She'd better hurry with the rest of her chores.

But when the dogs didn't stop barking, Penny moved to the barn door to look outside. A newer-model dual-cab pickup truck had pulled up near the front of the house. Penny didn't recognize it, and the driver had yet to open his door. As she

40

watched, her dad stepped onto the front porch and spoke a command that silenced the dogs. At last the driver got out and approached the house.

Since her dad didn't call for her to join him and the visitor, she turned back to the last of her chores. The cold was penetrating her coat, hat, gloves, and boots. One more reason to move a little faster. Still, it was another twenty minutes or more before she entered the house through the mudroom. She removed her outerwear, hanging her coat on a hook and placing her boots beneath it. In stocking feet she stepped into the kitchen. The aroma of coffee whirled around her, and she knew her dad had made a fresh pot for his guest. She grabbed her favorite mug and poured herself some of the hot, fragrant brew. At this time of day, she would have preferred hot chocolate with marshmallows, but the coffee was ready.

Male voices drifted to her from the living room. She followed the sound, curious to see who was with her father. She stopped in the entrance to the living room and looked toward the sofa. The first thing she saw was Tux, on the couch, curled up against the visitor's thigh.

Brad! Her heart raced at the thought. Her

gaze darted up from the cat to the man's face.

It wasn't her brother, of course, but for a moment she couldn't reconcile the truth. It took several more heartbeats for recognition to set in. When it did, she felt a new kind of chill travel through her. Her mind went numb. Her limbs refused to move. Her throat closed tight.

Him.

Trevor Reynolds put a hand on the cat to steady the feline before he stood.

It can't be. It can't be. It can't be.

He cleared his throat, perhaps waiting for her to speak first.

Get out. You don't belong here.

"Miss Cartwright," he said softly.

Two months ago, she'd slapped him. Shouldn't that have been enough to make him go away and stay away? To stay away forever?

Her dad said, "Come in and join us, Penny."

She broke free of the emotional chains that had held her still and kept her silent. "No . . . I . . . I'm going up to my room." She turned quickly and hot coffee splashed out of the mug onto her wrist, scalding the tender flesh. With a small cry, she dropped the mug. It clattered to the floor and broke into several pieces.

"Penny!" Her dad's voice seemed to come from far away.

Trevor Reynolds stepped to the opposite side of the entrance. "Let me help you," he said. He squatted on his heels and picked up the pieces of broken mug.

For the second time, Penny was gripped by inertia. She couldn't move or speak. All she could do was stare at him as he cleaned up after her.

He stood again. "I'll take this to the kitchen." He motioned to her hand. "You should run some cold water on that." Then he walked away.

She tried to summon the fury that had sustained her the day of her brother's funeral. It wouldn't come. Not a bit of it. Only sorrow remained.

"Pen —"

"Not now, Dad." The words came out as a whisper. "I . . . I need a few minutes."

Feeling stiff enough to break into pieces, just like the mug, she went up the stairs to her room. Once there, she sat on the edge of her bed. The burn on her wrist stung. She tried to focus on the pain rather than on the man downstairs. What was he doing here, so far from Nashville? Was he cruel as well as careless? There was no good reason for him to have returned to Kings Meadow.

Her brother had thought the world of Trevor Reynolds from the very beginning. Brad had met the country singer at a music festival in Utah. Trevor had been kind to Brad, answering his questions, encouraging him in his love of music and the drums. But she hadn't known until later that Brad and Trevor kept in contact after that first meeting. If she'd known, maybe she could have put an end to the deep friendship that had grown up between them in the years that followed. Maybe she could have steered her brother away from seeking a career as a drummer.

She closed her eyes, remembering the excitement in Brad's voice when he'd called her last January. *"He hired me, Pen. I'm going on the road with Trevor and the rest of his band."* She hadn't congratulated him. She'd met his announcement with stony silence. Then he'd added, *"This is the best day of my life."*

The best day of his life.

And it led to the last day of his life too.

Penny fell back onto the bed and stared at the ceiling, her mind suddenly as empty as her heart. Time passed, although she didn't know how long it was before a rap sounded on her door.

"Pen? Can I come in?"

"Sure, Dad." She sat up as the door opened. "Is he gone?"

"He's gone."

"What did he say?"

Her dad entered the room and sat on the chair in the corner near the window. "We talked about Brad, about their friendship." His voice dropped. "About the accident."

"Oh, Dad. He shouldn't have —"

"I asked him to tell me about it, Penny. It wasn't easy, on either of us, but he honored my request and he answered my questions."

"But why is he here?" she whispered.

"Did you forget Brad was bringing Trevor to Kings Meadow for Thanksgiving? He wanted us to know his friend. He wanted to show off his hometown and his family."

She smiled sadly. That was just like her brother.

Her dad cleared his throat. "One of the last things Brad did was ask Trevor to promise he would come to Kings Meadow. That he would spend some time here. Trevor says he's here to help us."

"Help us? Why would Brad ask that? Trevor Reynolds can't be any help to us except by staying far, far away. If it weren't for him . . ." She let the words trail into silence.

Her dad raked both hands through his gray hair as he sighed. "He doesn't know exactly why. Neither do I. But I'm sure your brother had good reasons." Unshed tears made his eyes glimmer.

"Oh, Dad." She rose from the bed and went to him, kneeling on the floor and pressing her cheek against his chest.

He stroked her hair for a long while, silence filling the room. But eventually his hand stilled and he said, "We owe it to Brad to discover why he sent Trevor to us. Your brother had a purpose. I know that much."

Another objection rose in her throat. She swallowed it back.

"God must have a reason as well for sending him here."

She sat back on her heels, her gaze meeting her dad's.

He leaned toward her. "Don't allow anger to take you hostage, my girl." He kissed her forehead. Then he stood and offered a hand to draw her to her feet. "Whatever the reasons are, I think you'd better get used to seeing Trevor around. I have a feeling he will be here for a while."

Get used to seeing him? She couldn't believe her ears. Get used to Trevor Reynolds being in Kings Meadow? Never. Not if she lived to be a hundred.

46

■ ■ ■ ■

The visit to the Cartwright ranch had gone both better and worse than Trevor had imagined. Rodney had been kind and polite. No, he'd been more than that. He'd seemed concerned for Trevor as they'd spoken of difficult things. There had been no blame on his face or in his eyes. Sadness, yes. Grief, to be certain. But no blame. Trevor had expected judgment, anger, possibly harsh words, and instead had been welcomed by Brad's father with the warmth of a long-lost friend.

However, Brad's sister was another story. Trevor had hoped her feelings toward him had mellowed over the last two months. It was obvious they hadn't. Perhaps they'd even worsened.

Back at his rental, Trevor went to work, getting the place in order. He unpacked the remainder of his clothes. The closet was barely adequate. However, the built-in dresser had ample space in its wide drawers. He left his guitar case in the corner near the faded green-and-red plaid sofa. Although he'd never been the sentimental type, he did have a framed photo of his parents at their fortieth anniversary party and another of him and his band that had been taken a couple of months before the accident.

Look at those grins.

Life on the road hadn't been easy all the time, but they'd loved playing together, the four of them. And their youngest member had fit right in from the start.

His chest ached as his gaze fastened on Brad. He'd really liked the kid. Loved him like a little brother. Maybe because Trevor had been a lot like him at the same age. Except for two things: Brad's faith and Brad's patience. Trevor didn't have much of either. And when it came to the career he had always wanted, he hadn't been willing to wait for his chance at stardom. He'd abandoned college and headed for Nashville at the age of nineteen, certain that it wouldn't take him any time at all to make it in the music business. Like about ten thousand other kids with a little talent and a lot of hope.

Trevor gave his head a slow shake and turned from the shelf where he'd set the photographs. No point running those memories through his mind again. Not even the good ones. Because if he kept it up, eventually he would find himself remembering painful moments too. His thoughts would churn as he considered ways he might have changed his present by doing or saying things differently in the past.

With determination, he completed his unpacking. Then, stomach growling, he took a package of hamburger out of the refrigerator and made his dinner.

Brad

2005

Brad was thirteen when he bought what the music store called a starter five-piece drum set. Nothing fancy. Just the basics. But as far as he was concerned, the toms and the snare and the rest were worth every penny he'd paid for them. He'd done extra chores around the ranch for his dad and had worked for a couple of neighbors to save up for the set of drums. Now, at last, they were his. And his dad had agreed to pay for drum lessons as long as Brad agreed to be in the junior high school band. Sure. Why not? It would just mean he could play more, even while at school.

When he and his dad got home from the music store in Boise, Brad moved his bed closer to the window and put the drums in the corner.

"Makes me glad I'm leaving for college in a few weeks," Penny said from the doorway.

He tossed a scowl in his sister's direction,

but she responded with a grin.

"Dad may be deaf by the time I get my degree. Maybe sooner than that." She stepped into the bedroom to give the drum set a better look. "Couldn't you have bought an acoustic guitar instead?"

Taking his seat on the stool, he answered, "Don't want to play the acoustic guitar." He took the pair of drumsticks in his hands. "Didn't you ever know there was something you just had to do? I'm supposed to play drums. I feel it in here." He touched his chest with a drumstick before tapping out a simple rhythm on the drums.

Penny reached to ruffle his hair with one hand. "Okay, buddy."

He wished she would stop doing that. Made him feel like a little kid, and he wasn't. Not anymore. He was already taller than her, and his voice was low enough that sometimes, when he answered the phone, the caller thought he was his dad.

"When do you start your lessons?" She took a step back, then another.

"Next week."

"Good. That means you don't have to practice now. Let's go for a ride along the river. We won't have many more opportunities before I leave."

I'm gonna miss you, Pen.

Something flickered in her eyes as she watched him, as if she'd read his thoughts. Truth was she often knew what he was thinking, almost before he knew it himself. Were all older sisters like that? He didn't think so. His friends even said he was lucky his sister was leaving for college. He didn't feel all that lucky. Penny had always been there for him, even before their mom died. Sure, she'd teased him plenty, and sometimes he thought her a royal pain in the backside. But mostly he loved her and knew she felt the same about him.

He set down the drumsticks as he rose from the stool. "Sure. Let's go."

Before Penny could respond, Brad darted around her and raced down the stairs. "Betcha I can get my horse saddled before you can," he shouted over his shoulder, ending with a laugh.

"Not a chance, buddy." She was hard on his heels by the time he flew off the porch. "That day'll never come."

Yeah, he was going to miss her plenty.

CHAPTER 3

Penny had always loved the Christmas season, particularly here in Kings Meadow. The commercialization of the holiday hadn't reached her hometown. Not like it had in most places. And she was grateful for it. Most folks hereabouts knew how to keep Christ in Christmas. Even those who didn't share the Christian faith. The town's decorations had gone up along Main Street the weekend before Thanksgiving. With the blanket of snow covering everything in sight, Kings Meadow was the twinkling, sparkling, picturesque winter wonderland people sang about in the month of December.

But this year would be different for Penny and her dad. The joy had gone out of the season before it had even begun. She didn't care if they had a Christmas tree, but she was determined to put one up anyway because her dad had made mention of it.

She would force herself to string lights and hang familiar ornaments on the branches. To please her father, she would even bake the traditional sugar cookies and decorate them, the way she'd done every December since she was a little girl.

The Cartwrights had received several invitations to join other families on Christmas Day for dinner. Again, Penny didn't want to but would go wherever her dad wanted. She'd left it up to him whose invitation to accept.

On her lunch break Penny bundled up in her down coat and knit cap and gloves and walked to the bookstore in town. The owner, Heather Kilmer, usually teased Penny, the librarian, for shopping in her bookstore. But not today. Today she simply smiled a greeting and asked if she could help.

"No. I'm just looking. I thought Dad might like a book for Christmas."

"Well, holler if you need me."

"I will."

Penny spent a good portion of time at work looking through catalogs of books she might buy for the library. There were way more books released every month than the Kings Meadow Library District could afford to acquire. And yet despite the hours she spent making those difficult decisions,

Penny still found pleasure in strolling the aisles of a bookstore, touching books, holding books, reading the back covers or the inside flaps. Her dad's favorite books — when he wasn't reading something new about beef cattle husbandry — were World War II histories and murder mysteries. Perhaps she would get him one of each.

She rounded an end display, expecting to see the shelves of the history section, only another shopper was in her way. She nearly collided with the man's back. "Oh." The word came out on a breath.

He turned, and when she saw his face, her heart sank.

Him again.

Trevor touched the brim of his hat. "Miss Cartwright."

"Mr. Reynolds," she answered stiffly.

"Call me Trevor. Please."

I don't want to call you anything. She turned to leave.

"You must be shopping for your dad," he said, stopping her planned escape.

She pressed her lips together as she faced him a second time. How could he not realize that she didn't want to be near him? That she didn't want to speak his name? How could he not see her feelings in her eyes or hear it in her voice?

55

His brief smile held a hint of sorrow. "Brad liked to haunt the bookstores in every town where we did a show, looking for history books that he knew your dad didn't have."

Fresh hurt stung her heart. She hated that this man knew something about her brother that she hadn't known. It felt as if Brad had betrayed their father.

And me.

Trevor glanced toward the nearest books. "I was hoping to find something on the history of Kings Meadow and the area."

Despite her wish to remain silent, she said, "Heather keeps those books up toward the front of the store."

"Thanks. I'll look there." He touched his hat brim a second time. "Appreciate your help." Then he walked away.

Letting out a rush of air, Penny leaned a shoulder against the bookshelves.

"Get used to seeing Trevor Reynolds around," her dad's voice whispered in her memory.

How could she get used to it when seeing him made her feel this way? Angry and sad and weak and speechless, all at the same time. This was *her* hometown. What right had he to come into it and ruin whatever semblance of peace she might manage?

56

■ ■ ■ ■

Trevor stared at several shelves containing the local interest books, but his thoughts were in the back of the store and on the pretty blonde woman with the beautiful, pain-filled blue eyes. Penny Cartwright looked so much like Brad. The siblings could have been twins, if not for the years that had separated them.

Penny blamed Trevor for her brother's death. She'd made that clear. And he could even understand why. He should have insisted that he and Brad stop for the night at a motel rather than pushing on to their final destination. A gallon of coffee couldn't have overcome the depth of exhaustion both men had felt that night.

For a moment, he relived the terror he'd felt as his shoulder slammed into the front seats, jarring him awake. Before he could understand what was happening, he'd been tossed up, then down, then up again. Grinding, screeching, breaking sounds had deafened him. And then everything had stopped with an abruptness that stole the air from his lungs. Silence, followed by pain.

With iron resolve, Trevor forced the memories back into a deep, dark corner of his mind. He ignored the aches in his body that still plagued him and drew in a deep breath through his nostrils. He let it out slowly through parted lips.

Better. That was better.

He reached for a book on the shelf at eye level and thumbed through the pages, scanning chapters and old black-and-white photographs without actually seeing them. Finally, he carried several books to the counter, paid for them, and left the bookstore.

He paused on the sidewalk and checked his watch. Almost one o'clock. He had an appointment at one thirty to interview for a part-time job as a town maintenance man. From what little he'd been told about the position, it sounded perfect for him. One day he might be cleaning up at the high school after a tournament and the next blowing snow off the sidewalks along Main Street. And since it was part time, it would leave him free to do what he could to fulfill his promise to Brad.

He turned right and set off walking in the direction of the mayor's office. Kings Meadow, he'd discovered, wasn't difficult to navigate. Streets tended to wind a bit rather than being laid out in straight lines, but they still ran in mostly an east-west or a north-south direction. Block sizes weren't uniform, but that gave the town character.

Christmas decorations glimmered in shop windows along the way, reminding Trevor that he needed to do some shopping for his mom. She had urged him to come home to California for the holidays, but he'd declined. His heart told him Kings Meadow was where he needed to be this year. The belief didn't make complete sense to him, but for a change he was going to pay attention to that small voice inside of him.

It wasn't long before the mayor's office came into sight. It was a single-story building made of white brick, perhaps the size of most of the two-bedroom homes that had been built in the forties. When he opened the door, he heard a small electronic beep, alerting the two employees working in the front office that someone had entered. The woman at a desk off to the right didn't bother to look up from the papers before her. The younger woman behind a long counter smiled in welcome.

"May I help you?" she asked.

He walked toward her. "Yes. I'm Trevor Reynolds. I have an appointment about the maintenance position. But I'm early and can wait."

"I'll let Ollie know you're here."

59

Trevor had barely taken a seat on one of the chairs before a man came out of the office in the back. He was a big man, in both height and width. With the exception of the plaid jacket he wore over a blue shirt above boots and jeans, the man bore a striking resemblance to a character in an old movie about mountain men.

"Mr. Reynolds." The man's bushy white-and-gray beard brushed against his collarbone. He thrust out a hand. "Pleasure to meet you. I'm Oliver Abbott."

Abbott? His meeting was with the mayor?

Trevor stood. "Nice to meet you, sir." He took the man's hand and they shook.

"Come into my office so we can talk." The mayor motioned toward the open door beyond the counter.

On what planet does the mayor interview for a maintenance position? Trevor swallowed a chuckle and followed Mayor Abbott into his office.

The next half hour was interesting. Ollie, as he insisted on being called, didn't seem interested in Trevor's skills with a hammer, screwdriver, dust mop, or snow blower. Especially not after he learned Trevor had made his living as a musician for the past thirteen years.

"I love country music, and I love to sing,"

Ollie said, leaning back in his chair. "But I never had a knack for playing any musical instruments. I envy people like you. You know, we had a young fella here in Kings Meadow who —" Abruptly, he stopped talking. His eyes narrowed, then widened again as he put two and two together. "Brad Cartwright was your drummer." His affable smile was gone.

"Yes." *And there goes the job.*

"Does Rodney know you've come to town?"

Trevor nodded. "I was out at his place a couple of days ago."

Ollie steepled his fingers in front of his mouth, the pads of his index fingers tapping slowly. His eyebrows, as bushy and white as his beard, drew closer together.

Trevor heard the muffled voices of the two women in the outer office, then the closing of a file drawer. A large clock ticked off the seconds on the wall behind the mayor. Maybe he should leave. Why draw out an interview that would go nowhere?

But before Trevor could rise from the chair, Ollie lowered his hands and gave an abrupt nod of the head, as if having made up his mind on something. Trevor wished he'd left of his own volition before the mayor could dismiss him, but it was too late now.

"Can you start work on Monday?" Ollie said.

Trevor was tempted to knock the side of his head a couple of times and ask the mayor to repeat himself. He managed to subdue the impulse, instead saying, "Yes. Yes, I can."

"Good." Ollie stood.

Trevor followed suit.

"We'll have some paperwork for you to fill out on Monday, and then Yuli Elorrieta — Yuli's the public works supervisor — he'll show you the ropes." Ollie put out his hand once again. "Welcome to Kings Meadow, Trevor."

"Thank you, sir. I appreciate it."

A short while later, he stood on the sidewalk in front of the mayor's office. His gaze went toward the heavens. What were the odds, in a town this size, that he would find a place to rent the same afternoon he arrived and then get the first job he interviewed for? He was no mathematician, but he was certain the odds were great against either of those things happening. And for both to happen to one guy?

I guess You really did mean for me to come to Kings Meadow, God. Brad always said You care about the small details as well as the big. I guess that's true. Now if You could just help me figure out what I'm supposed to do here, I'd be grateful. Real grateful.

Rodney stared at the computer screen, the heels of his hands resting on the desk, fingers lightly touching the keyboard. Opening the e-mail program hadn't been difficult, but clicking on the link that would open the mailbox named "Brad" was proving problematic. Every time he reached for the mouse, his chest tightened. He hadn't looked at e-mails to and from his son since the day Brad died. But it seemed important that he do so now.

It had been two days since Trevor Reynolds came to the ranch to talk to him and Penny, and in those two days the promise Brad had extracted from the singer had never been far from Rodney's thoughts. His son had had the gift of discernment. He'd cared about and accepted people wherever he found them, then had drawn them closer to God by being a loving friend. Brad had sent Trevor to Kings Meadow out of love. Rodney understood that much.

He clicked the mouse, looked at the long list of saved e-mails to and from his son — dating back to his first year in college —

and scrolled to the one he'd received soon after Brad moved to Nashville.

Dear Dad,

You're not going to believe this. At least I can't believe it. Not that it happened this fast, anyway. I got to audition for Trevor Reynolds, and he hired me. Maybe I'm that good or maybe it's because Trevor and I have become friends through e-mail over the years or maybe it's because I'm so inexperienced he can pay me less than he'd have to pay others. Whatever the reason, I'm now employed as a drummer in a band. We'll be going out on the road in less than three weeks.

Nashville's been a little hard to get used to. It's so big compared to Kings Meadow. Even compared to Boise. Everything moves faster too. But I'm going to like it. I'm sure of it.

This would sound crazy to lots of people, but I know you'll understand. I don't think God brought me to Nashville just so I could play my drums, even though He delights in giving good gifts. I think I'm here to help Trevor in other ways. He doesn't know Christ, first off, and from a few things he's said I guess his dad was rough on him. Maybe even knocked him around when he was a kid. Anyway, they weren't close like you and me, and I've got the feeling Trevor doesn't care much for the idea of a heavenly Father because he never knew what a loving dad could be like. He's a good guy, but he's got a wounded spirit.

Dad, please tell Penny how much I love her. We didn't part on the best of terms, but you already know that. Tell her I'm sorry I disappointed her but that this was what I had to do. I hope one day she'll see that.

Take care of yourself. I hope your back's not giving you too much grief.

Love you,
Brad

Rodney drew a shaky breath and let it out slowly. He remembered reading this e-mail almost a year ago, but Brad's words hadn't made the impact on him then as they did now.

Lord, help me honor my son's last request. Thank You for sending Trevor to us. Help me know the right things to say and do while he is here in Kings Meadow. Holy Spirit, mend this young man's heart.

After taking another breath, he clicked on

the next e-mail in the list and began to read
again.

BRAD

2007

On the first night of winter church camp, a fire burned bright in the lodge's stone fireplace, but the heat from the flames didn't reach all the way to where Brad sat, second row, left side of the room. Kids were there from six different churches, seventh graders up to seniors in high school. Brad's first year at winter camp, he hadn't mixed much with kids he didn't know already. Instead he'd hung out with his best friends from Kings Meadow and been content to do so.

But this year he'd come to the opening session ahead of his roommates and had settled onto a chair surrounded by students from a church in Boise. He recognized most of them from the previous year. But it wasn't their familiarity or the church they attended that drew him into their midst. It was something else. He just couldn't say what. It was simply a feeling that he needed to be there. A strong, deep-down feeling he couldn't ignore.

The guy on his right introduced himself — Mark — then asked a few sociable questions. Normally, Brad wasn't comfortable in get-acquainted situations like this one. There wasn't a lot to say about himself. He wasn't involved in team sports, although he enjoyed watching football. He was a good student and liked to read. He liked to hang out with the friends he'd known all his life but steered clear of the kinds of things that had gotten some of them into trouble. His favorite thing to do was play the drums and he dreamed of being good enough to be in a band someday. But for some reason, he was at ease with Mark and didn't mind answering the older boy's questions.

As more camp attendees filled up the rows of chairs in the lodge, the worship team made its way onto the small stage. After a few minutes of tuning guitars and adjusting speakers, they began to play. Softly at first. Then young people around the room began to rise to their feet and sing along. Words for the song appeared on an overhead screen.

Brad closed his eyes, a strange feeling stirring in his chest. A feeling he couldn't put a name to. Something he'd never felt before, that was for sure.

It wasn't as if the worship song — and then the next one and the next one — was unfamiliar to him. The church he'd attended his entire life, beginning in the nursery at two weeks old, sang contemporary worship songs as well as old hymns. He'd been around plenty of people who talked about God on a regular basis. But even so, something was different tonight. Or maybe it was an expectation that something was about to change.

That *he* was about to change.

CHAPTER 4

The Kings Meadow Annual Christmas Bazaar was held on the first Saturday in December. For the past three years, Penny had been in charge of the event. She'd been thankful for the volunteer job this year. It had kept her from dwelling on Brad's death, at least some of the time. Today she was especially glad for it. There was a wonderful sense of community in the fellowship hall of the Methodist church, and it warmed her heart, made her feel almost whole, even put her in a little bit of the Christmas spirit. Perhaps it was seeing so much creativity in one place that did it.

Buck Malone and Antton Zubiar had a table full of leather goods. Plus they were holding a raffle for one of Buck's hand-crafted saddles, with all of the profits going to the food bank.

Bling was Skye Nichols's forte. Her booth featured handmade jewelry. Everything in it sparkled in the light that fell through the windows, threatening to blind people as they browsed.

Several women from Meadow Fellowship Church had a quilting booth, and the quilts hanging on the wall behind their counter were nothing short of stunning.

There was a booth with dolls and toy trucks, another with handmade baby clothes, and another with a plethora of knitted and crocheted goods.

The bazaar wasn't missing plenty of yummy food items either. Shoppers had choices of cookies, candy, pies, and cakes. Nothing like trying to gain the first couple of holiday pounds three weeks before Christmas.

The thought made Penny smile . . . just before she took a bite of a giant-sized snowman cookie. It tasted even better than expected. Food had held little appeal to her the past two months. It was a nice change to bite into something and discover enjoyment again. She continued to nibble on the cookie while she strolled around the room, ready to help if help was needed.

Her smile returned, even broader this time, when she saw Ollie Abbot enter the fellowship hall wearing a Santa hat on his head. With those woolly eyebrows and that beard of his, the mayor of Kings Meadow could pass for the jolly old elf with no trouble at all. But that plaid jacket would have to go.

As if drawn by her smile, Ollie walked straight toward her. "Another successful bazaar, I see," he said.

"It seems to be."

"It's a lot of work, I know, but you don't look the worse for wear."

"Thanks." *I think.* She chuckled to herself.

"The missus says she gets half of her Christmas shopping done at this annual bazaar. Lots easier than that drive down to Boise and a day at the mall."

"Mom used to say the same thing."

"Yes, she did." Ollie's gaze scanned the room. "Is your dad here?"

"Not yet, but he should be soon."

Someone tapped on Penny's right shoulder. She looked to see who it was.

Krista Malone, one of the high school principal's daughters, said, "Mom needs an extension cord for the adding machine. The outlet isn't working where it's plugged in now."

"I'll see to it right away, Krista." Penny looked at the mayor again. "Please excuse me."

"Sure. Sure. You go on. I know you're busy."

Fortunately, Penny knew where to look for an extension cord, and she was back in the fellowship hall with a couple of them a few minutes later. She took them to the long table near the exit that served as the checkout counter. As she plugged one of the cords into the wall, she made a mental note to tell Reverend Butler about the faulty outlet.

When she straightened and turned, the first person she saw was Trevor Reynolds as he came through the entrance doors.

What is he *doing here?*

Oddly enough, her good mood didn't vanish completely at the sight of him. Which didn't mean she was glad to see him either. Only that the infusion of Christmas spirit was strong enough to keep less pleasant feelings at bay. Still, it might be best to give him a wide berth.

That thought had no more than crossed her mind when he noticed her. A faint smile curved the corners of his mouth. She wondered if he might come over to speak to her and was glad when he turned toward the nearest booth.

That's a relief.

She watched as he browsed items on the display.

"Who is *that*?" someone whispered near her ear.

Penny glanced over to see Tess Carter, the daughter of the local dentist, standing beside her. Tess's gaze was locked firmly on Trevor as he moved to the next booth. Penny wanted to ignore the question but couldn't. "His name is Trevor. Trevor Reynolds."

"Where has he been all my life?" Tess flicked a strand of loose dark hair behind her shoulder, then looked at Penny. "Do you know him? Could you introduce me?"

The last thing in the world Penny wanted to do was play matchmaker for Trevor Reynolds and Tess Carter. Tess was a nice girl, a friend since elementary school, but a total flirt. As for Trevor . . . Penny wanted him to have more reasons to leave Kings Meadow than reasons to stay. "Sorry. I don't really know him." The words were accurate, if not entirely true.

Tess laughed softly. "Well, I'm not going to let that stop me. Happy holidays, here I come." With a backward wave over her shoulder, she headed into the crowd of shoppers.

For a moment, Penny envied Tess. She had one of those sparkling, charismatic personalities and never seemed afraid to plunge into a new social situation. She took meeting new people in stride, and men fell for her with hardly a glance. Of course, Tess's personality hadn't guaranteed her happiness. She'd fallen in love and married at twenty-three but had been divorced by her twenty-sixth birthday. She'd returned to her hometown to, as she put it, lick her wounds.

It must have worked. She looks fabulous.

Before Penny could mull over that thought for long, she was summoned to another booth and presented with another problem to solve. Both Tess and Trevor were soon forgotten.

Trevor bought twenty raffle tickets at the leather goods booth. He didn't need to win a custom-made saddle, as he hadn't owned a horse in over five years. But the money was going for a good cause. After writing his name and his landlord's phone number on half of each ticket, he dropped them into the large glass fishbowl and stuck his half into his pocket. As he turned toward the next booth, he nearly collided with a young woman.

"Sorry," he said, taking a short step backward.

She laughed. "My fault. I was intent on

that gorgeous saddle." She tilted her head slightly to one side. "I don't think I know you. I'm Tess Carter." She offered her hand.

"Trevor Reynolds." He gave a nod as he spoke, then shook her hand.

"It's nice to meet you, Trevor. Have you been in Kings Meadow long?"

"No. Not long."

Tess Carter had a pretty smile, and something in her manner said she knew how to use it to her advantage. "I'm dying to know what brought you to our little town. It's off the beaten path, you know."

"I needed a change of scenery," he answered.

Her dark eyes widened, inviting him to say more.

He gave her one of his own smiles instead. He knew how to use them too.

After a few moments of silence, she asked, "Are you shopping for anyone in particular?"

"My mom."

"You're sure to find something for her. Would you like me to show you around? I know pretty much everyone here."

Not exactly subtle. But why not agree? It couldn't hurt anything, and he'd always appreciated the company of women. Especially a woman as vivacious and attractive as Tess Carter.

The next hour proved more successful on the Christmas shopping front than he'd expected when he entered the church hall. Tess's company was more delightful than he'd anticipated as well. As she'd stated, she knew almost everybody, and she made a lot of introductions as they worked their way from booth to booth. By the time Trevor was ready to pay for his purchases, he no longer felt a complete stranger in town.

A pleasant-looking, heavyset woman in her fifties added up his items, then ran his credit card through a charge gizmo on an iPad. Another woman put everything into bags. Within no time at all, he was ready to leave.

He looked at Tess, who had waited at the end of the table. "Thanks, Tess. It was a real pleasure."

"For me too." She held out a slip of paper. "Here's my phone number, in case you ever want some friendly company. It isn't like there are a lot of entertainment options in Kings Meadow. Especially this time of year."

He took the paper and stuffed it into his shirt pocket. Then he bid her a good day and walked out through the doors marked

Exit. He was halfway down the hallway when he saw Rodney Cartwright and his daughter standing beside a coatrack, deep in conversation. Penny's shoulder almost touched Trevor's coat that hung nearby. He'd bet good money she would move if she knew it belonged to him.

As Trevor approached, Rodney glanced up and smiled a genuine welcome. Penny turned. Her smile had gone AWOL.

Rodney said, "Looks like you had a successful morning."

"Yes, sir. I did. My Christmas shopping is pretty much done." Trevor looked at Penny again. "I heard you're in charge of this bazaar. Great job."

"Thanks."

Could she have sounded any less pleased by the compliment? He doubted it.

"I'd better go back in, Dad." With a silent nod in Trevor's direction, Penny walked away. He watched until she disappeared into the fellowship hall, then his gaze returned to her father.

Rodney said, "This isn't easy for her."

"I understand that, sir."

"She misses her brother a lot. We both do."

So do I. But even as that thought crossed his mind, he knew he didn't feel the same loss as Brad's father and sister. Trevor had lost a friend he'd known well for only a matter of months. The Cartwrights had lost a young man they'd loved all his life.

"Are you sorry you came to Kings Meadow?" Rodney asked, intruding on Trevor's thoughts.

"No." He said the polite thing and then realized he'd spoken the truth. He was glad to be here. Despite arriving less than a week ago, he'd already discovered a certain charm about this small town tucked away in the mountains. No doubt part of the reason was the affection Brad had felt for it. When Trevor and his band were on the road, scarcely a day had passed that the youngest member of their group hadn't shared a story about his dad or his sister or an old schoolteacher or the woman who ran the bed-and-breakfast or one of his lifelong friends.

"You'll see for yourself when you go with me for Thanksgiving," Brad's voice whispered in Trevor's memory. *"You're going to love it there."*

Trevor hadn't held out much hope he would take to a place. Any place. He didn't have a lot of good memories of the place where he'd grown up. It was just another city on the map, his boyhood home just another house on the block. He knew that was because of his father, a man incapable

79

of giving or receiving love.

Rodney cleared his throat.

Jerked back to the present again, he said, "Sorry. What did you say?"

"I heard you've been hired on part time with Public Works."

"How'd you hear that? I haven't even had my first day on the job yet."

Rodney chuckled. "It's a small town, Trevor. News travels fast."

"I guess." Brad had warned him of that, but it still surprised him.

"The mayor's a good friend of mine," Rodney added.

"Ah."

"He took a liking to you. I could tell."

Trevor couldn't help but grin. "He's a colorful character, isn't he?"

"That he is. Ollie is one of a kind. One of a kind." Rodney glanced beyond Trevor's shoulder. "I think I'd better get in there before everything is picked over. One of the ladies makes the world's best fudge, and I still hope to get some."

"Good luck." Trevor reached for his coat.

Rodney took a couple of steps away, stopped, and turned. "Why don't you come for dinner tomorrow?"

Trevor almost agreed, but thought better of it. "Maybe you should talk to Penny

80

about that first. We both know she's not crazy to have me around."

"I suppose you're right." Rodney didn't smile, but there was something warm in his expression regardless. "Come after dinner, then. Say around two o'clock. I'll show you around our place."

"Okay. I'll be there."

Rodney nodded and turned a second time.

As Trevor watched the older man walk away, he realized how much he wanted to get Penny Cartwright to accept him — or at least not to hate him. If her father didn't blame him for Brad's death, maybe Penny could learn to feel the same. Of course, it might help if Trevor didn't sometimes still blame himself.

"They're gonna . . . need your help."

Trevor held his breath, resisting the memory, not wanting to think about those last minutes of Brad's life. Both of them had known he was dying, but Brad had spent those minutes thinking about others.

"Promise you'll go . . . Not just for . . . Thanksgiving. Go and . . . stay awhile. God will . . . show you what to . . . do. Just . . . ask Him."

With a shake of his head, Trevor strode toward the exit.

81

■ ■ ■ ■

Before entering the fellowship hall, Rodney paused to look behind him. Something stirred inside his chest as he watched Trevor leave the church. Because his son had liked the singer so much, he was prepared to like him too.

Help me care for him as You care for him, Lord. Show me all the reasons You brought him to us. Help me honor my son's friendship with him.

He released a breath and continued through the entry door. A quick sweep of his gaze located the candy booth, and he set off in that direction. He hoped he wasn't too late for some of Edna Franklin's fudge. His disappointment would be acute if he was.

He'd almost reached the booth when his daughter moved into his path, forcing him to stop. "Dad, you know the doctor said you need to cut back on sweets."

"Cut back, not cut out altogether. There are limits, dear girl, to what I'm willing to give up this side of heaven."

"Dad . . ."

He frowned. "I'm not in my dotage, Penny. Please don't treat me as if I am. And

I don't need you to act like my mother either." The look in her eyes said he'd hurt her feelings, and he regretted his words, even though he'd spoken the truth. "Sorry, honey, but I can still think for myself." He leaned forward and kissed her forehead, hoping the gesture might soften his added comment.

I know, she mouthed as he stepped back again. Then she gave him a fleeting smile before walking away.

His daughter was worried about him. And not just about him. Penny seemed to worry about everything. She tried her best to command the events around her, fighting hard to never lose control. Rodney had seen signs of the trait after the death of her mother, but it had worsened in recent years. And after Brad died . . .

He gave his head a shake, driving off the thought. If he wasn't careful, he would find himself doing exactly what Penny did. Instead of worrying, he chose to say another silent prayer, this one for his daughter, asking God to heal her heart.

"Merry Christmas, Rodney."

He looked to his right and watched Joe Dodson, the contractor he'd worked for off and on for many years, close the final steps between them. "Same to you, Joe. Haven't

83

seen you around much. How are you?"

"Good, thanks. And you?" The man's eyes said it was more than a casual question, more than an inquiry about the state of his health.

"I'm all right, Joe. Some days are better than others, but I'm doing all right."

"Glad to hear it." Joe looked away at the sound of someone calling his name. "Looks like Sue's done shopping." His gaze returned to Rodney. "I'm wrapping up a job down in Boise. When it's done, I'll give you a call."

Rodney nodded before his friend hurried after his wife. Then, resolute, he faced the candy booth once again. It wouldn't be the Christmas season without at least one square of Edna's fudge, and he sure hoped he wasn't too late to get it.

Hours later, Penny dropped onto a folding chair, exhausted. "Over for another year," she said to herself, then groaned.

"Everything ran like clockwork, Penny." Janet Dunn sat on another folding chair nearby. "You have amazing organizational skills."

"Must be the librarian in me." Penny was too tired to laugh at her own comment.

"You could be right about that." Janet

looked toward the opposite end of the fellowship hall. A tender smile curved her mouth and her face shone with love.

Penny didn't have to look to know the cause. The Reverend Tom Butler and Janet — both of them in their forties and never married — had recently become engaged. *About time too.* They had been dating for around two years, and anybody with eyes had known, long before this, that they belonged together.

"Have you and Tom decided on a wedding date?"

Janet looked at her again, smiling. "Am I that obvious?"

Penny managed to laugh this time. "Yes."

"Well, to answer your question, no." Janet shook her head. "We haven't decided yet. But we're considering Valentine's Day."

"Romantic. Can you plan a wedding that fast?"

"We can. It won't be anything fancy. Just family and a few close friends."

Penny nodded. That's what she would want, when she found the right guy. *I hope it doesn't take me until I'm forty.*

She was immediately ashamed of herself for the thought.

Janet rose. "I'd better go see if Tom needs any help."

Forty wasn't old, Penny reminded herself. And even if it was, it would be better to wait until forty than to rush into marriage with the wrong person.

That made her think again of Tess Carter's hasty, ill-fated marriage. Which — against her will — brought her thoughts back around to Trevor. Had he and Tess hit it off? They must have. Tess had stayed beside him the entire time he shopped. Not that Penny had paid attention to that particular detail. But as she'd moved about the room, she couldn't help but notice them together, both of them tall, both of them smiling, both of them attractive.

Attractive? Trevor Reynolds?

Well, yes. She had to admit — again against her will — that he was a handsome man. Even more so than in the photograph on his album cover, Stetson covering his dark hair, a Western scene behind him, that smile of his —

"Give him a chance," Brad had said to her the last time they spoke on the phone. *"Once you meet him in person you're gonna understand why I love working with him. He already likes you, I've talked about you so much."*

Her heart pinched at the memory.

And that was Trevor's fault too. If he hadn't come to Kings Meadow, if he would have stayed far, far away from her brother to begin with . . .

Just leave. Just go away. Please go away.

CHAPTER 5

Trevor considered attending the Methodist service his first Sunday in Kings Meadow. He'd learned Rodney and Penny were members there. It would have guaranteed his seeing them at least once each week. But at the last minute he chose to attend Meadow Fellowship, a non-denominational church on the west side of town. Something inside of him said his Sundays needed to be more about him and God and less about him and the Cartwrights.

By the time the service ended, Trevor knew this would be the church he attended as long as he was in Kings Meadow. Nobody had to tell him that his Christianity — if he'd even been a Christian — had been a superficial thing. Knowing Brad had slowly made him aware of the difference between calling himself a Christian and truly being one. Maybe that was one reason he'd kept his promise to Brad. Maybe it was here that his faith, such as it was, could grow.

Trevor had met quite a few members of the congregation at the Christmas bazaar the previous day, and it surprised him how many of their names he remembered. Living a life on the road, he'd rarely seen anybody two days in a row, other than the members of his band. He found he liked this fledgling sense of community.

He received three invitations to Sunday dinner before he exited through the church doorway. He declined each of them. It would be rude to eat and then rush off in order to be to the Cartwright ranch by two o'clock. So he returned to his studio apartment, where he warmed up some leftovers. He tried not to think about what he might have been eating if he'd accepted one of those invitations.

When he next looked outside, two o'clock drawing closer, the blue skies from early that morning were gone. The wind had begun to whistle around the corners of his apartment. A strong gust rattled the windows. He left his Stetson on the hook by the door and reached for the knit cap and scarf his aunt had made for him a couple of years back. Still, he wasn't prepared for the extreme drop in temperature that had happened while he was inside.

The streets of Kings Meadow were extra quiet on this Sunday afternoon, and as far as he could tell, only a few stores were open along Main Street. At least no Christmas shoppers were in sight when he stopped at the stop sign. All he heard was the mournful wind and the rumble of his truck's engine. Loneliness wound around his heart, and he realized that despite how friendly people had been to him at church that morning, he wasn't a part of that community — or a part of any other community. By his own choice, he'd kept himself from forming close relationships through the years. Brad Cartwright had been one of the few people who had found a way through Trevor's defenses.

He turned his truck east and drove beyond the limits of town. Snow began to fall when he was about halfway to the ranch. Tiny flakes, carried sideways by the wind, obscured his view and forced him to go even slower, afraid he might miss the turn. But he didn't miss it. Despite the snowstorm, the way felt familiar to him.

Arriving at the ranch, he parked in front of the house, got out of the pickup, and hurried up the steps to the front porch. He rang the doorbell and waited. The door was opened a short while later by Penny. Her expression was one of grudging resignation. She didn't want him in her home, but because of her father she wouldn't turn him away.

Did I think I could win her forgiveness in a matter of days?

Yes, in some ways, he supposed that was what he'd thought. Most women believed he had charm to spare. Plenty found him good looking and talented and fun to be around. But none of that mattered one iota to Penny Cartwright. It was clear as day. In her cool blue eyes. In the stern line of her mouth. In her rigid stance.

"Come in, Mr. Reynolds," she said, frost in her voice. "Dad's waiting for you."

He wanted to remind her to call him Trevor, but he swallowed the words as he stepped into the house while removing his knit hat. Penny closed the door and then silently held out her hands to take his coat after he'd shrugged out of it. She placed it on the coat tree and his hat and scarf on a nearby table.

Her dad appeared in the doorway to the kitchen. "Trevor, glad to see you could make it. How are the roads?"

"Not bad."

"Care for something warm to drink before we brave the elements?"

"Sure."

"Coffee okay?"

Trevor nodded.

The older man waved him forward before turning and moving out of sight. Trevor followed, thinking to himself that Rodney was like his son in many ways. Brad had had an affable, hospitable nature too. No one had been a stranger to him. At least, not for very long. He'd had true empathy for those around him, no matter who they were. And when Brad had spoken of his family back in Kings Meadow, his love for his dad and sister had been obvious.

By comparison, Trevor's relationship with his father had always been troubled, cold, and distant. After he left for Nashville, on those rare occasions when he'd spoken with his father by phone, there had always come a moment when his father would ask, "When are you going to get a real job? When are you going to make something of yourself?"

His father had passed away a number of years ago, but the memory of those questions remained a pinprick to Trevor's heart. With practiced resolve, he pushed the thoughts away and let his gaze roam the room, looking for something to keep his thoughts from returning to those uncomfortable memories.

The kitchen in the Cartwright home was large and airy. The breakfast nook had bay windows that looked out on a fenced pasture where several horses stood, backs to the wind and snow. While Rodney filled two large mugs with coffee, Trevor crossed to a curio cabinet in one corner. Behind the glass were family photos, china and crystal, knicknacks, and a large collection of thimbles.

"The thimbles belonged to my wife, Charlotte." Rodney stopped on Trevor's left. "Some of them are rather valuable, but I can't bring myself to sell them. She enjoyed them so much." He held out the mug of coffee.

Trevor took it. "My mom collects those lighted villages."

"Where do your parents live?"

"A small town in Northern California. But it's just my mom now. My father died a few years ago."

"Sorry to hear that."

Trevor accepted the words of condolence with a nod.

After that, the two men stood in silence as they drank their coffee.

Penny held her breath, listening from the

hallway, but neither her dad nor his guest said anything more. Fearing she might get caught eavesdropping as they left the kitchen, she quietly moved to the living room, where she stopped and stared out the window at the snowstorm.

She didn't like the feeling that coiled in her stomach, and it wasn't difficult to identify it: jealousy. Like her brother before him, her dad had taken a quick liking to Trevor Reynolds, and she didn't want him to. They were acting like friends. Didn't her dad understand that Trevor had taken Brad from them?

"Honey?"

She turned toward her dad's voice.

"Trevor's going with me to feed the livestock. Want to come along?"

"Shouldn't you wait until the storm lets up a bit?"

Her dad pulled on his coat, followed by his gloves. "Maybe it will by the time we're finished in the barn."

Penny knew she should be glad her dad had help. He'd become an advocate of feeding his cattle three times a day after reading a study that showed increased weight gain in three feedings versus the same amount of feed given once or twice a day. But she thought the extra work was too much for

94

him. He wasn't as strong as he used to be. His back caused him a lot of pain, though he tried to hide it from her, and he tired easily.

"I'll be out in a few minutes," she answered at last, choosing not to repeat her concerns just now.

Her gaze slipped to Trevor, standing beyond her dad. She could see that he watched her, but the dim light in the entryway prevented her from reading his expression. Unsettled, she looked out at the snowstorm again. Moments later, she heard the door open and close.

She was reminded of last Christmas when Brad had been home. It had been a good holiday for all of them. How many times had she watched the two people in the world she loved the most bundle themselves in coats and hats and gloves and head out into the frigid elements to tend the livestock? Seeing father and son together had made her happy. Her brother had spent the days helping their dad with anything and everything that needed doing, and Penny had envisioned things going along the same way for years to come. Brad, she'd believed, would find employment with an engineering firm in Boise, and the rest of the time he would be at the ranch, helping their dad.

Then, two days after Christmas, her brother had dropped his bombshell: He wasn't staying in Kings Meadow. He wasn't looking for work in Idaho. He was leaving for Nashville to audition as a drummer for a band. If he got what he was hoping for, he would be going on the road with Trevor Reynolds.

Less than nine months later, he was dead.

Tears welled, but Penny refused to let them fall. Anger served her better than sorrow, she reminded herself. With a determined tilt of her chin, she headed for the mudroom, where warm attire awaited her. A short while later, ready for the elements, she headed outside, walking with head down toward the barn.

The door squeaked as she opened and closed it. Just inside, she stopped, giving her eyes a moment to adjust to the dim light. Then she moved toward the sound of her dad's voice. He and Trevor stood side by side, forearms resting on the top rail of the stall that held Harmony.

"When's the foal due?" Trevor asked.

Before her dad could answer, Penny said, "Late March or early April."

Both men turned toward her.

Trevor said, "She's a beautiful horse. I've always been partial to buckskins."

The same was true for Penny, but she wasn't about to say so to him. She didn't want to sound as if they had anything in common.

"Well," her dad said, intruding on her thoughts, "let's get the cows fed." He turned and headed for the rear door of the barn.

Parked outside was an ancient flatbed truck that her dad somehow managed to keep running from year to year. On the bed were bales of hay and, in a makeshift rack behind the cab, a couple of pitchforks. Penny went straight to the back of the truck and hopped onto the bed. Trevor followed close behind and mirrored her action while her dad got into the cab. Moments later, the engine roared to life. In unison, Penny and Trevor moved to the front of the bed and grabbed hold of the railing. As they drove toward the pasture where the cows awaited them, the wind died down and the falling snow turned to fat, lazy flakes that drifted to earth, catching on knit caps and eyelashes.

"It's beautiful here," Trevor said above the rumble of the truck.

"Mmm."

"Brad always said Kings Meadow is the most beautiful place in the world, but I

97

figured he was prejudiced. Now I'm not so sure."

Penny followed his gaze to the nearby mountains, the green of pine trees dappling the snowscape. The tension that had been coiled so tightly inside of her eased a bit. Maybe it was hearing that her brother had talked about Kings Meadow with affection. When he'd turned his back on Idaho in pursuit of a different kind of dream, it had felt like a rejection of all that her parents had loved. All that Penny loved too.

The mooing of cows interrupted her thoughts.

Trevor laughed. "I guess they know what's coming."

Without answering — or waiting for the truck to stop completely — she hopped down from the bed and hurried to open the wide gate. Her father drove the truck through the opening, and Penny swung the gate shut again, then got back onto the bed. The truck followed a slow, circular route, and Penny began cutting twine and shoving the bales off one side of the bed. Trevor watched a moment and then joined in, shoving hay off the opposite side. She could see that he was strong, and he worked fast. When their gazes met again, he grinned, seeming to enjoy the physical labor.

"Is this how all ranchers feed their cows?" he asked.

She gave a little shrug. "Depends on the operation, the size of the herd, the location, the weather, and the preference of the rancher. Mostly the latter. This is how Dad's always done it."

"He loves this ranch. That's obvious." His smile broadened.

Is this how you charmed Brad into working for you? With that smile of yours and that easygoing manner and knowing just the right thing to say? With those silent questions, she willed her irritation with him to return. She succeeded . . . a little.

"Black Angus, right?"

"Yes."

"Beneath the frozen mud stuck to their coats, they're a pretty animal, aren't they?"

His comment surprised her.

"Don't *you* think so?" Trevor asked with another of his effortless smiles.

She wanted to remain irritated with him, but how could she be annoyed after he said something like that? She'd always thought her dad's cows were pretty. Especially the ones raised for 4-H, after they'd been bathed, brushed, and curried and were ready to be judged at the fair, their black coats gleaming in the sunshine. And their calves were beyond cute. Penny loved watching them gambol about the pasture in the springtime. Every year there was one that became her favorite.

"Yes," she answered at last. "I think so."

Trevor broke the twine on the last bale of hay and shoved the feed off the truck. As soon as she saw him step back from the edge, Penny rapped on the roof of the cab three times to let her father know they were done. The truck completed its wide circle, stopping once more at the gate. This time Trevor jumped to the ground before Penny could, and he was the one who opened the gate. He grinned at her as the truck rolled past him, his enjoyment obvious.

Mercy, he was much too handsome — and he knew it too. It was easy to imagine girls hanging all over him after a concert. He must have his choice of beauties in every town he and his band performed in. But he wouldn't find that kind of attention here in Kings Meadow. Women in these parts had more sense than that.

Then she remembered Tess Carter at the bazaar yesterday, and her confidence in female friends and neighbors drained away.

Well, at least I have more sense than that. She frowned to herself. *Was that what Brad liked about the life of a musician? The atten-*

tion of women? She gave her head a slight shake, knowing that wasn't true of Brad. He'd liked girls, of course, but his enthusiasm about music, especially about the drums, went back to before he'd noticed the opposite sex.

"Thanks for letting me help," Trevor said. "I enjoyed it."

She drew back, surprised to find him standing on the truck bed beside her. She'd been so lost in thought she hadn't noticed he'd rejoined her or that the vehicle was moving once again.

Wordless, she shrugged.

He looked as if he would say something else, then nodded and let it pass.

Thank goodness for small favors.

BRAD
2008

The summer between Brad's freshman and sophomore years in high school, he got a part-time job as a bag boy at the Merc. He had his eye on a fancy new drum set, and there was no way he wanted to earn the money doing chores around the ranch. That might have been okay when he was thirteen. It wasn't okay anymore.

He was bagging groceries for Sophie Anderson when he saw his sister enter through the automatic doors. His face broke into a smile that matched hers. "I thought you weren't coming home until tomorrow," he said as she drew closer.

"I couldn't wait." Penny kissed his cheek and lifted a hand as if to ruffle his hair, then thought better of it. She looked up at the two women on either side of the checkout counter. "Hi, Ms. Cook. Hi, Mrs. Anderson."

"Another year of college under your belt?"

Laura Cook asked as she rang up the final item on the conveyer belt.

"Yes. Three down. Three to go."

"Getting your master's, I take it." Sophie Anderson slipped her debit card from her wallet. "Good for you. What in?"

"Library science."

"Penny the librarian," Brad said, rolling his eyes. "Doesn't sound very exciting."

"It's what interests me, buddy. It'll be a good career."

Brad liked to read, but he didn't care for the idea of spending his life inside some stuffy old library. He had bigger dreams than that. Or maybe just different ones. Had Penny ever wanted something different? Something that involved stepping out on a limb? Taking a risk?

"I'd better let you get back to work," she said, intruding on his wandering thoughts.

"Okay. I'll see you at home in a couple of hours."

Penny bid good-bye to the other women, ending with a little wave that took in all three of them. Then she left the grocery store.

"Your sister has blossomed into a beautiful young woman," Laura Cook said as she handed the paper receipt to Sophie Anderson. "I wouldn't be surprised if she found a husband before she gets that master's degree."

Brad gave a slight shake of his head. If that's what Ms. Cook thought, she didn't know Penny Cartwright. When his sister set a goal, she didn't waver from it. She made her plan and then stuck to it. She'd been like that as far back as he could remember. Maybe she didn't look strong because of her slender figure, but she had a will made of pure steel. No guy she met would be able to alter the plan she'd made. Brad would wager on it.

CHAPTER 6

Trevor took an immediate liking to his supervisor, Yuli Elorrieta. The middle-aged man was short and slight of build. He had a hooked nose that seemed too prominent for his narrow face, but his smile came easily and there was a twinkle in his eyes that said he enjoyed life to the fullest degree possible. A photograph on the desk in his office suggested a large number of children and several grandchildren as well.

On Monday, Trevor's first day on the job, Yuli gave him a walking tour of Kings Meadow. "Our department takes care of street maintenance and cleaning. We're responsible for maintaining all of the town-owned properties." He pointed out three of those as they walked west on Main Street. "We clean the storm drains, put up and take down the holiday decorations at Christmas and for the Fourth of July. Public Works is also in charge of trash pickup within the town limits. Residents who live outside the limits have to take their trash to a collection area on the southeast corner of town. We'll drive over there later."

"Okay."

"Our department takes care of the sidewalks, including snow removal, and we also maintain and install street signage."

No answer seemed required, so Trevor nodded to show he continued to listen.

"Since you're a part-time employee, it's doubtful you'd ever be called in for an emergency, and you won't be assigned to any one particular task as our full-time employees are. When you check in each workday, you'll get your assignment for that day."

"Sounds simple enough."

"It should be."

They completed their loop in silence, arriving back at Yuli's truck. They got in and headed, as promised earlier, toward the trash collection site.

As Yuli drove, Trevor asked, "How long have you been the supervisor of Public Works?"

"Twenty years come January."

"Wow. Twenty years? That's a long time in one job."

Yuli chuckled. "I've been employed with them even longer than that. Went to work for the department when I was still in high school. Working part time, like you are now."

"And you never left?"

"No."

"Not even for college?"

"No. My family had little enough money to spare for the essentials in life. My father considered college a luxury." He glanced over at Trevor. "You?"

"I attended a small college in California right out of high school, but I was too eager to break into the music business to last in it for long." He turned his gaze out the passenger window. "I regret it sometimes."

"Maybe you should do it now. It's never too late." Yuli laughed softly. "As soon as our youngest daughter graduates from the university, it's going to be my turn."

Trevor's eyes swung back to Yuli. "You're going to leave your job for college?" *At your age?* he finished silently.

"I won't have to leave. I'll take classes online." The older man grinned. "It's a different world we live in today."

Trevor thought of his father. How disappointed he'd been when Trevor left college. But then, Trevor had disappointed William Reynolds all his life. Nothing Trevor had achieved as a boy or as a man had been good enough for his father. No grade had been high enough. No award grand enough. No job good enough. No girlfriend pretty enough.

They arrived at the trash collection site, and Trevor was thankful for the interruption to his thoughts. Yuli pulled the truck into the lot and stopped but left the engine running. He pointed out the different containers and explained the duties performed by the employees. Then he put the truck into gear and steered the vehicle back toward town, following a different route that would bring them, he explained, to the large metal building that housed the Public Works vehicles and equipment.

They'd traveled little more than a quarter of a mile when they saw a blue sedan parked on the side of the road, its right wheels buried up to the hubs in snow, the driver peering into the open trunk.

Penny Cartwright, Trevor thought, recognizing the coat she wore.

"Looks like she has a flat tire," Yuli said, slowing the truck and moving to the side of the road.

Penny heard their approach and turned around. Her blonde hair was hidden beneath a sky-blue knit cap. Her coat covered everything but the hem of her skirt, a flash of dark tights, and knee-high boots. Not all that much to see, and yet he thought she looked adorable.

Her smile revealed relief and she waved at Yuli. But when both men got out of the truck and she recognized Trevor, the smile faded. Although he knew he needed to be patient, he was tired of that reaction. Couldn't she cut him a bit of slack?

"Looks like you could use some help," Yuli said to Penny.

"I can, yes. I'm expecting an important telephone call at the library, and I'm running late." She waved toward the open trunk. "It's been a decade since I changed a tire. I'm not sure I know how to use the jack."

Yuli chuckled as he turned toward Trevor. "Do you know Miss Cartwright?"

"Yes, we've met," he answered, deciding not to add that he'd pitched hay off the back of a truck with her the previous afternoon.

"Good. You take the truck and deliver Penny to the library. I'll meet you there as soon as I change the tire."

Trevor didn't have to look at Penny to guess her opinion of that suggestion. "I could stay and change the tire," he offered. "Why don't you drive —"

"No. No. Go on with you. I'll be there in no time." Yuli stepped to Penny's side and

109

looked into the trunk. "Everything I need is here," he added a few moments later.

"All right. You're the boss." Trevor's gaze shifted to Penny. "Let's go, then. Don't want you to miss that important phone call."

It frustrated him, her continued reluctance to have anything to do with him, but he did his best not to let it show. He'd hoped that the time they'd spent together yesterday would ease some of her dislike for him. Couldn't she give him a chance to prove he wasn't a bad guy?

With a curt nod, she opened the door of her car and retrieved her purse and a briefcase. A steady *ding ding ding* let everyone know the keys were in the ignition. She closed the car door, silencing the sound. Then she walked toward the passenger's side of the truck. Trevor sprang into action, beating her there in time to open the door and offer her a hand up.

"I can manage," she said, ignoring his offer of help. She tossed purse and briefcase onto the seat ahead of her and proved her point as she climbed into the high cab with surprising ease.

Of all the men in Kings Meadow who could have come down the road at this hour of the morning, why did it have to be Trevor

Reynolds — in the truck with Yuli Elorrieta — who'd stopped to render aid?

"Are you late to open the library?" he asked, starting the truck's engine.

"No. Karli, my assistant, will be there already. She comes early on Mondays." She turned her gaze from him to the road ahead. She could at least be glad that the flat tire had happened only minutes away from the library.

Trevor didn't try to force a conversation between them, and they drove the rest of the way to the library in silence. But instead of pulling up to the front of the building and dropping her off, as she'd expected, he parked the truck and turned off the engine. As he opened his door, he said, "I figure I might as well get a look inside while I wait for Yuli. And it wouldn't hurt for me to get a library card while I'm here."

He was like a bur stuck in a horse's mane. So difficult to be rid of. And so irritating while it remained, tangling the hair the way it seemed he tangled her life.

With a sigh, Penny got out of the truck and led the way to the entrance of the Kings Meadow District Library. Trevor reached for the door before she could, opening it and allowing her to go through first. She started toward her office, but as much as she wanted to give him the cold shoulder once again, she felt compelled to stop and look back at him. "Thank you, Mr. Reynolds."

"Trevor."

She released another sigh. "Thank you, Trevor. I'm grateful for the lift."

"Yuli did the cold, hard work." He punctuated the words with one of his slow grins.

For a second, she felt unable to think, let alone move.

"So where do I go to get a library card?" he asked.

She managed to point toward Karli behind the counter.

"Thanks. I'll see you later." He walked away.

She remained where she was for a few moments. Then she felt her face grow hot — and she didn't even know the reason for it. Ducking her head, she hurried into her office and closed the door.

Why do I let him get under my skin?

She went to her desk chair and sank onto it.

Penny Cartwright was not a woman who swooned over handsome men like some silly secondary character in a Regency romance. Looks had never been the first thing that drew her attention to members of the opposite sex, not even as a teenager. She responded to intelligence, to rational left-brain thinkers. And if that kind of man was someone with a ten-year plan for both his professional and personal lives, all the better.

So why was it that just looking at Trevor made her heart run a little faster? What was it about his smile that made her stomach whirl in an oddly enjoyable fashion?

She didn't even *like* him, for pity's sake! He was a second-rate country singer. If he was first rate, he'd have been playing bigger venues. She would have heard his voice on the radio. Right? Worse still, musicians like him were vagabonds. Definitely not people who kept a ten-year plan. And besides, he hadn't finished college. She knew that from Brad. Maybe Trevor hadn't been able to hack academics. How bright could he be, living the way he did?

But he doesn't seem unintelligent, does he?

Rising from the chair with a groan of frustration, she shrugged out of her coat and carried it to the coat tree in the corner near the door. Her knit scarf she poked into the right sleeve of her coat. Her gloves went into a pocket.

The phone rang as she was returning to her desk.

"Penelope Cartwright," she answered in an all-business voice, grateful for anything that would turn her mind from unwelcome thoughts about an even more unwelcome singer from Nashville.

Half an hour later, Penny placed the handset in its cradle and rose from her chair. The call had been productive, but her head was swirling with new information and a slew of ideas for how to implement them in their library. A cup of hot coffee was in order, the stronger the better. She left her office and hurried toward the back of the building. A woman on a mission, as her mom used to say.

Karli Hellman — a friend since junior high and the only other full-time employee of the library — was turning away from the coffeemaker as Penny entered the break room. "Great minds," she said, lifting her full mug a little higher.

"I know." Penny retrieved her own over-sized mug from the cupboard.

"Mr. Elorrieta came in and left your car keys. I knew you were still on the phone, so I stuck them in the far right-hand drawer behind the counter."

"Thanks." Penny poured coffee into her mug.

114

"And I helped Mr. Reynolds get his library card. He seems nice."

"Mmm."

"Do you know him well?"

Penny turned toward Karli. "No, not well."

"Ah." Disappointment laced the single word. "I thought, since you came in together . . ." Karli let the comment drift into silence.

"He was a . . . Mr. Reynolds was a friend of Brad's."

"Oh, Penny. I'm sorry." Karli's expression changed from curious to stricken. "I wouldn't have said anything if I'd known."

"It's okay, Karli."

"No, it isn't. I see how much it hurts whenever anybody talks about your brother." Karli stepped away from the break room counter. "I'd better get out front."

Penny nodded, glad to put an end to their conversation.

She was aware, of course, that many of her friends and neighbors had taken to walking on eggshells around her. She could tell they didn't want to mention Brad for fear of upsetting her. They saw her as fragile, breakable. But she would disagree with them if they said it to her face. She grieved, but she wasn't weak. And besides, it wasn't fair to Brad's memory never to speak of him. He was beloved by many. He should be remembered. Remembered often.

A lump formed in her throat.

Maybe I am a little *fragile.*

Trevor's image intruded on her thoughts.

Perhaps I've been a little unfair to him as well. Maybe he wasn't entirely at fault for what happened to Brad.

Maybe so . . . but she wasn't ready to admit it yet.

Seated in his easy chair, Rodney awakened with a start, uncertain how long he'd been asleep. He believed in power naps, but he didn't hold with drifting off to sleep while upright in his chair. It usually left him with a crick in his neck and a grumpy humor.

But he didn't give thought to any stiffness or mood this time. He'd been dreaming of Brad. One of those dreams that felt real. A dream that didn't slip away too quickly to remember. He could recall it all. His son had been seated on the top rail of the pasture fence, boot heels hooked on a lower rail, a long piece of straw held between his teeth. The sun had been shining. The grass had been green.

Rodney had walked to him, overjoyed by

his presence. *"When did you get home?"* he'd asked.

Brad had smiled as he removed the straw from his mouth. *"Not long. I brought Trevor with me. He's got a good start, Dad. He's trying to change the way he thinks, the way he lives. But you need to help him the rest of the way."*

"Be glad to, son." Rodney had nodded. *"Be glad to."*

Rodney rose from his easy chair and walked to the window in the kitchen, looking out at the fence and the pasture that had been in his dream. He couldn't say whether or not God had given him a vision or if the dream had only been helping him realize something his subconscious already knew. Whichever it was, Rodney was convinced that God was going to do a work in all of their lives. From out of the ashes He would bring beauty. And it would begin with Rodney loving Trevor the same way he'd loved his son.

"Lord, that young man thinks he's here to help me and Penny in some way," he whispered. "Maybe so. Maybe that's part of it. But I think it's just as much about us helping him. Helping him know You better. Helping him know what it means to be part of a loving family. Helping him find his way in his new faith. Show me how I'm to make all that come to pass." He took a breath and released it. "Amen."

BRAD
2008

Brad's border collie, Queenie, had her first litter of puppies on Christmas Eve. The family's usual holiday routine, upon returning from the candlelight service at church, was completely forgotten as Brad, Penny, and their dad observed the birth from the hall outside the laundry room. Any one of them was ready to step in if the dog appeared to be in distress, but the first-time mother took labor and delivery in stride, giving birth to a half dozen healthy puppies without complaint.

"Look at this one," Penny said now as she cradled one of the newborns in the palms of her hands. "It has a lot of brown on its face. Kind of a ginger-brown shade."

Brad couldn't remember a time when the Cartwrights hadn't owned at least two border collies, sometimes as many as four. All of their ranch dogs had been black with varying degrees of white markings. There'd

never been one with brown markings anywhere in the mix.

"That's what we'll have to call it." Penny
held the puppy up a little higher. "Ginger."

"If you have a Ginger," his dad said,
"you're going to need a Fred too."

"Who's Fred?" Brad asked.

His dad laughed softly. "You know, Fred
and Ginger. Like the dancers in those old
movies I like to watch."

Brad failed to understand, but it was
easier to just act like he did. "You don't even
know if Ginger's a girl." He took up another
mewling puppy. "But if it is, then we'll call
this one Fred."

"If it's a boy," his dad and sister added in
unison.

Brad knew right then that he wouldn't be
selling Fred or Ginger, no matter their
genders. These two would remain on the
ranch for their whole lives. With his dad's
help, he would train them, the same way
he'd trained Queenie and Queenie's parents.

An image of his mom, kneeling beside a
box full of puppies, wafted through his
memory. He could barely recall her face
without the help of photographs, but he
remembered her hands as she'd held one of
the puppies. Hands with long, narrow

fingers and a gentle touch. The way she'd drawn it close and rubbed its coat against her cheek. And the dogs had always loved her in return. In fact, they'd been obedient to all the family, but they'd been most devoted to his mom.

He glanced up at his dad. Was he remembering something similar? Could be, judging by his wistful expression.

"Come on, you two," his dad said. "Time we were all in bed. Santa won't come if you're still awake."

Brad and Penny exchanged a glance. Their dad had said similar words to them every Christmas Eve for as far back as they could remember. And it didn't seem to matter that neither of them had believed in Santa for over a decade. He just went on saying it. Brad wouldn't admit it to his sister, but he hoped their dad never stopped saying it. It was tradition now.

He put the black-and-white puppy into the clean bed with Queenie and its siblings. Penny followed suit a moment later with the ginger-faced pup. Then they both rose from the floor and headed for their upstairs bedrooms, Penny wrapping an arm around Brad's waist. She used to wrap it over his shoulder, but he was the taller one now.

"That's something I miss when I'm at college," she said as they stopped in the hallway outside of her bedroom.

"What?"

"Seeing the baby animals born. Calves. Colts. Puppies. Kittens. Chicks. I didn't realize how much I loved being surrounded by all the new life until I was away from it my first year." She gave his waist a squeeze before taking a step closer to her doorway. "I'm glad I was here for this."

Brad thought he was too old to get all mushy and sentimental with his sister. So he swallowed the threatening lump in his throat and gave her a nod to say he was glad too.

She smiled. "See you in the morning."

"Pen?"

"Yeah?"

"You're all right. You know that?"

"I love you too, buddy. I love you too."

CHAPTER 7

The first telephone call that Trevor received on the newly installed telephone in his apartment was from a man he'd met at Meadow Fellowship the previous Sunday. Chet Leonard, he'd already learned, was the largest land-owner in the valley. Others had told Trevor that Chet and his wife ran a successful quarter horse operation year-round and some sort of luxury dude ranch in the summer and early fall.

After identifying himself, Chet said, "I know this is late notice, but Rodney Cartwright mentioned you might like to join a group of men in a Bible study. We gather on Thursdays at seven o'clock in one of the Sunday school rooms at Meadow Fellowship. I think you may have met a few of the men, in addition to Rodney."

"Rodney attends? But I thought he went to the Methodist church."

"Oh, he does. The men in the study attend different churches and a couple don't attend any church . . . yet. We just happen to meet at Meadow Fellowship."

Trevor was tempted to decline, but he hadn't been back to the Cartwright ranch since Sunday afternoon. His second week in Kings Meadow had been busier than expected, getting the hang of his new job and, with the use of his landlord's telephone, tying up a few unexpected loose ends back in Nashville. Attending the study would be an opportunity to remind Rodney why Trevor had come to Idaho, if nothing else.

"Okay. Sure. I'll be there."

"Terrific. Bring your Bible and a notebook if you want. See you at seven."

"Yeah. See you then."

After hanging up the phone, Trevor glanced at the clock on the stove. He had better than an hour before he would need to leave. Plenty of time to fix himself a quick supper.

By the time Trevor left his studio apartment, night had fallen over the valley. An inky-black darkness that residents of large cities never experienced. The Christmas lights on Main Street twinkled from lampposts and storefronts, giving the small town a fairytale appearance, and he couldn't help but smile, knowing he'd worked on a few of those light strands this week.

There were four trucks and one minivan parked in the lot beside Meadow Fellowship when Trevor arrived a few minutes before seven. He got out of his pickup, held his almost brand-new Bible to his chest, and hurried toward the entrance. Once inside, the sound of voices drew him in the direction of the classrooms off to the left of the sanctuary.

"Here's Trevor now," Chet said upon seeing him.

Rodney Cartwright was the first to shake his hand and begin making introductions to the men already seated in a circle of chairs. As Chet had indicated, a few of them Trevor had met already. Not surprising, he supposed, in a town of this size.

A short while later, with everybody settled into place, the young man — Adam Carlton — who sat opposite Trevor took a guitar from behind his chair and began to strum it while singing. The other men joined in. All of them seemed to know the words to the song. Trevor didn't, so he was content to listen. At first he found himself critiquing Adam's performance. The young man's voice was on key but not strong, and his guitar playing consisted of only a few repeated chords, although that served as enough to keep the rest of the men in tempo.

But as the song continued, Trevor began to listen to the lyrics. They were words of worship and praise, a kind of love song to Jesus. Simple and full of trust. After a while something shifted in his chest. He couldn't have described the feeling if his life depended on it, but he believed God was in the midst of this circle of men. He closed his eyes, both shaken and soothed by the unexpected encounter.

It's about Me tonight. No one but Me.

It was Trevor's own voice he heard in his head, yet the words didn't feel like his own thought. Once again he had the feeling he was in the presence of something beyond himself. *Someone* beyond himself.

The song came to an end. With the last chord still reverberating in the air, Chet began to pray. Like the song before it, the words of the prayer were simple, filled with love and trust. Different from the lofty kind of prayers Trevor had often heard in public gatherings. It made him think of Brad. The kid had had a quiet but strong faith. Brad had never hesitated to answer questions anybody asked about his beliefs, and he'd never seemed offended when those asking the questions weren't quick to agree with him. He hadn't joined other members of the band in drinking or womanizing as they traveled from gig to gig, and yet nobody had felt judged by him either. How had he managed to carry that off?

Chet's "Amen" drew Trevor out of his musing. When others grabbed their Bibles, so did he. Chet told the group to open to a chapter in Romans. Trevor was thankful he at least knew Romans was in the New Testament, although it seemed to take him too long to find the right place. The never-opened pages seemed to stick together in groups of twos and threes.

A glance at Rodney Cartwright's Bible proved the same couldn't be said of it. The open pages — obviously well read — had many highlighted and underlined passages. Handwritten notes filled the margins: top, bottom, and sides.

Chet began reading the designated passage. Trevor's translation was slightly different, but he was able to follow along.

As the other men in the Bible study began to discuss the passage in Romans, Rodney remembered something his son had said in one of their last telephone conversations.

"Dad, Trevor's a little rough around the edges, but he's got a good heart. He's so hungry for God."

Rodney glanced toward Trevor and realized that God was already answering the prayer he'd whispered a few days ago. It was as if Brad's friendship with the singer had been transferred into Rodney's heart, full and complete. Deep and unexpected affection for Trevor washed over him.

One after another, he recalled things his son had told him, both in e-mails and when they talked on the phone. Mostly stories about Trevor. The kindnesses he had shown toward others. The words of encouragement he'd spoken to Brad. The loneliness that came with being on the road so much of the time. The times Brad had awakened and couldn't remember what town or city they were in. And eventually, the questions Trevor had begun asking about what Brad believed, about his faith.

Rodney was startled when he heard Chet begin the closing prayer. How had he allowed his thoughts to wander for the entire discussion? Had any of the other men noticed his lack of attention? He feared it would have been hard for them not to notice.

A short while later, as the group began to

break up for the night, Rodney turned toward Trevor. "Did you enjoy the evening?"

"Yes." Trevor shrugged. "I got lost in some of the discussion. I can't claim to know my Bible well."

"That comes with time, son." He put a hand on Trevor's shoulder. "And remember, following Christ is a lifelong journey. Christians are foot soldiers, so to speak. Always on the march. Always learning. Always growing stronger."

Trevor grunted. "I hope you're right."

"I am." Rodney stood, and his back gave him a painful twinge. He rubbed the sore spot with his left hand.

Trevor noticed. "Sir, I don't work tomorrow." He rose too. "I thought I'd come out and help feed the cows and whatever other chores you might have for me. In fact, if you'll let me, I'd like to help with at least one of the feedings every day. On my days off, I could do more than one."

It was on the tip of Rodney's tongue to refuse. But another spasm jabbed his back and he thought better of turning down the offer. As much as he would like to pretend he was a young man with a strong constitution, he could use the help. And if the two of them were to be of help to each other, what better way than spending more time together? "Sure," he answered at last. "I'd be grateful for your help. Like the old saying goes, many hands make light work."

"What time would you like me to come over?"

"Penny helps in the morning before she goes to work. Why don't you come at one?"

"One it is. I'll be there."

At the sound of the back door closing, Penny looked up from her knitting, surprised when she saw the time.

"Dad?"

"Yes, it's me." He appeared in the living room doorway.

She put the needles and yarn into a nearby basket to protect them from Tux, who delighted in unraveling unguarded knitting projects. "I didn't realize how late it is. How was your Bible study?"

"Good. But it's always good." He entered the living room and sank onto his recliner with a deep sigh. "Always good to be home too."

Did he look more tired than usual? "Can I get you anything?"

"No. I'm fine. But not sure I'll manage to stay awake for the news. It's been a long day."

He *was* more tired than usual. "Dad, now

130

that I'm back to work, why don't you feed the cows just once a day? Or even twice a day."

"I've told you why." He shook his head. "I'll go back to a single evening feed for calving season, but for now I want to stick with three times a day."

"But it's so much extra work for you."

Her dad's expression changed from tired to exasperated. "Pen . . ."

She raised her hands in defeat. "Okay. I won't say anything more about it."

"You know what I could really use?"

"What?"

"To see you having a little bit of fun. You should spend your free time with others your own age. Accept some of those invitations you get from your girlfriends. Go to a dance or a movie or just out to eat. You don't need to sit around with your old dad all the time."

"I *like* spending time with my old dad."

He leaned toward her, resting his forearms on his thighs. "Penny, you should get to *be* young while you *are* young."

Go out. Have fun. Meet a nice man. Go on a date. Fall in love. Get married. Have babies. She heard all of that in her dad's simple comment. But it felt wrong that she had those options when her brother could never

131

do any of them. Rationally, she knew it wasn't wrong to want those things. But she couldn't reason away the feelings. They were inside of her, tangled up with grief and guilt.

With another sigh, her dad rose from his chair. "I think I'll call it a night after all." He stepped over to the sofa, leaned down, and kissed the top of her head. "Good night, Pen. I love you."

"I love you too, Dad. Sleep well."

She listened as he climbed the stairs to his bedroom. After his door closed behind him, she considered retrieving her knitting once again, then decided against it. She suddenly felt as tired as her dad had looked.

CHAPTER 8

Penny leaned forward for a better view of the computer screen. "There," she told Bill Carter, seated at the keyboard. "Click on that button."

"That's why I couldn't figure it out." He chuckled. "It was too easy. Thanks for your help."

"No problem." She straightened and turned away.

The library seemed extra quiet today. Karli Hellman was off on Fridays, Tara Welch was busy shelving books, and there were only three patrons in the building, two of whom were nestled in opposite corners of the stacks, reading books. Only the soft clatter of Bill Carter's typing on the keyboard broke the deep hush. Penny returned to the back side of the checkout counter and began sorting through the paperwork that never ended.

Sometime later, she felt the whoosh of air

that announced the opening of the front entrance doors. A quick glance at her watch told her that over half an hour had passed. She looked up to see Tess Carter leaning down to kiss her dad's cheek. Then Tess headed straight for Penny.

"Just the girl I wanted to see," she said, smiling that unforgettable smile of hers.

Penny cocked an eyebrow and waited for an explanation.

"A bunch of us are getting together tonight to play board games at my dad's house. Totally spontaneous and last minute, and it's up to me to make sure we've got plenty of victims. Er . . . I mean guests." She laughed at her own joke. "Will you come? Eight o'clock. I promise you'll have a good time. You'll know everybody who's there."

"Oh, Tess, I don't know if I —"

"Please. We'd really like you to come."

"Penny," she heard her dad say, *"you should get to be young while you are young."* And maybe he was right. It had been good to return to work. It had been good to see people at the bazaar. It might be just as good to spend an evening with friends playing silly games. She drew in a slow, deep breath. "Okay. I guess I could make it."

"Terrific!"

"Should I bring anything?"

"Nope. Not a thing. Got it covered. I've already bought enough snacks and beverages to last all night."

All night?

Tess laughed again. "Don't look so horrified, Penny. I can't imagine anybody will last longer than midnight or one. Especially the married ones who have babysitters to pay."

Penny released a breath.

"Okay. Gotta run." Tess waggled her fingers in a mini wave, then in an exaggerated whisper tossed in the direction of the public computers, said, "Bye, Dad. See you later."

By the time the doors closed behind Tess, Penny already regretted her decision to go to the Carter home. She'd never been much into board games, although when she and Brad were young, the family had been known to enjoy some rip-roaring card games. Spoons had been their mother's favorite.

I could call her and say something came up and Dad needs me at home tonight.

No. No, she couldn't say that. It wouldn't be true, and her dad would hate it if she involved him in such a lie. No, she would go to Tess's impromptu party. She'd kept too much to herself since Brad's death. Her father was right about that.

Tara Welch pushed a now-empty cart from out of the stacks. When she drew close to Penny, she said, "The returns are all shelved, Miss Cartwright."

"Great. I'm going into my office to eat my lunch and finish writing my Christmas cards. Call if you need me."

"Sure thing."

Penny retrieved her sack lunch from the fridge in the break room — half of a tuna salad sandwich, a dill pickle, a low-fat yogurt, and a diet soda. It didn't take long to finish her light meal, and as soon as she was done, she got to work addressing envelopes and adding personal notes to the Christmas cards.

She'd planned to skip sending cards this year. But then Christmas greetings from friends far and near had begun to arrive. They'd collected on a side table in the living room, so many filled with words of love and encouragement, until Penny had known she couldn't ignore them any longer.

Her own words were few: *Thanks for thinking of us this Christmas* and variations on the same theme. A few times, memories of Brad and their childhood Christmases caused tears to well in her eyes and she had to stop writing while she blinked them away.

Suddenly she was glad she'd accepted Tess's invitation for tonight. Her dad was right. She needed this. For weeks the preparations for the Christmas bazaar had taken up every spare moment. Now that it was over, she had too much time on her hands, despite her work at the library. She would go tonight and play games and find reasons to laugh.

So help me, I will.

Trevor was just about to leave his apartment when his telephone rang. The sound startled him. It wasn't like a lot of people had his number. He hadn't even told his mom yet. And he doubted it was Chet calling again.

"Hello?"

"Hi. Trevor? It's Tess."

"Tess?"

"Well, that's not very flattering." She laughed airily. "Tess Carter. We met last weekend at the Christmas bazaar. I didn't think you'd forget me that fast."

"Sorry. Of course I didn't forget you. I was just surprised you had my number. The phone's new."

"Well, that's a relief. I hate to be forgotten. And just so you know, I got your number from your landlord. Listen, a bunch of old friends are getting together tonight at my dad's house to play board games and eat junk food. Eight o'clock. We would love for you to join us."

"I don't —"

"You already know at least two of us. Me and Penny Cartwright. And I'm sure you've met a few of the others over the last couple of weeks."

The news that Penny would be present at the gathering gave him pause.

"Please join us, Trevor. You'll have a good time. I promise."

He pictured Penny as he'd last seen her, rushing into her office at the library, hurrying to escape his presence. Tess Carter, on the other hand, desired his company. Why not join in? He wasn't in Kings Meadow to become a hermit.

"Okay," he answered her. "I'll come." He reached for a pen and the nearby notepad. "Give me your address and some directions."

A short while later, as he drove toward the Cartwright ranch, he wondered why he hadn't been the one to call Tess during the past week. He had her number; she'd given it to him on Saturday. She was single, pretty, and obviously interested in him. What could it hurt to see if they might hit it off?

When Trevor arrived at the ranch, the two border collies greeted him from the front porch. Just a couple of barks and a pair of wagging tails. Obviously, Fred and Ginger had accepted him into their midst, as had their master.

But will the master's daughter ever come around? The jury was still out on that one.

He took the steps up to the porch two at a time and knocked on the door.

Rodney answered soon after. "Hey, Trevor. Step inside. I need to get my coat and gloves." He glanced at the border collies. "Good dogs."

Fred and Ginger went to their sheepskin beds, coiled in slow circles, and lay down with matching groans. Trevor chuckled as he stepped into the house and closed the door.

"It was good to see you at the men's study last night." Rodney pulled on his coat and fastened the front.

"I'm glad I went, sir. First time I've ever been in a group like that." He shrugged. "It was different, but I liked it."

"Good. That's good."

"Brad studied his Bible a lot. The guys and I gave him a hard time about it at first, but later on . . ." He fell silent and shrugged again.

Rodney said nothing, just watched and waited.

"He's the one who bought me that Bible I brought with me." *Not that I opened it much until last night.*

There was great patience in Rodney's eyes, a look that encouraged Trevor to say more, a look that said he was in no hurry to do anything else as long as Trevor might want to talk.

And surprisingly, he found himself wanting to say more. "Brad was different from anybody I've ever known before. I mean as a Christian. His faith . . . what he believed . . . It wasn't a Sunday kind of thing." The comment made him think of his father. William Reynolds had gone to church some Sundays, but he'd spent the rest of the day badmouthing the sermon, the music, and the people in the pews. Even as a young boy Trevor had wondered why his father went if he hated everything that much, if it didn't somehow make him a better man for it. "If I'm going to be a Christian," he said softly, "I want to be the kind that Brad was."

The look that crossed Rodney's face was bittersweet. Pain and joy mingled together. Finally, in a voice hardly more than a

140

whisper, he said, "You could not have paid my son a better compliment, Trevor. Thank you for telling me."

Trevor nodded.

The older man must have sensed the momentary confession had come to an end. He started to pull on his gloves, and as he did so, the telephone rang. "One minute." He held up his index finger. Then he disappeared into the kitchen.

Trevor heard another sound and felt something rub against his legs, first one shin, then the other calf. He glanced down as the cat stopped its serpentine walk between and around his legs. She looked up at him and meowed. He tried to remember her name, but it escaped him. He was about to lean down and pick up the feline when Rodney reappeared in the kitchen doorway.

"Sorry about that," he said. His gaze lowered to the cat, and a moment later he smiled. "Until you came to the ranch, Tux never took to anybody other than Brad. But she likes you. I hope you don't mind her. Not everybody likes cats."

"They're all right, I guess. I've never had any pets of my own."

"Never?" Rodney pulled on his work gloves.

"My dad was allergic to almost everything." *Sometimes I thought he was allergic to me.* "After I left home, I traveled too much to have a dog or cat. I owned a horse when I was in school and had another one after moving to Nashville. But like I said, I travel too much, so I sold him to somebody who'd be able to ride him."

They headed outside. The day was cold, the sky a brilliant blue. Sunlight sparkled off the crusty snow. Trevor was quick to put on his sunglasses. Rodney simply tugged his hat brim lower on his forehead.

Fred and Ginger ran ahead of them, slipping into the barn through the partially open doorway. Rodney paused long enough inside the barn to check on the two horses in their stalls. Then they went out the barn's back door and loaded bales of hay onto the flatbed truck before driving out to the pasture. They did it all without much in the way of conversation. Trevor found it a comfortable silence. As if they'd been doing work like this together for years.

It made Trevor think of his father once again. They hadn't known a comfortable moment together since Trevor had been a little kid. And their relationship had worsened after he abandoned college for a career as a singer. With his father's passing, any chance of Trevor finding a way to change

142

things between them — if he'd even wanted to — had ended too.

As he broke bales apart and tossed the feed to the cows, he let himself envy the relationship Brad had enjoyed with his dad. Similar to Trevor's father, Rodney Cartwright hadn't been overjoyed when his son left Kings Meadow, abandoning the idea of a more conventional career to live a vagabond existence as a drummer in a moderately successful country band. But Brad's choice hadn't driven father and son apart. Not even for a moment. On the contrary, it may have even drawn them closer together, according to Brad.

Trevor remembered the snatches of one-sided phone conversations he'd overheard, sometimes in the van or a car as they followed a highway across one state or another, sometimes in a motel room or while waiting for a meal to be delivered in a restaurant. Whenever Brad had spoken to his dad or about his dad, there'd been a smile on his face and in his voice.

Lucky guy.

Trevor tossed the last of the hay off the back of the vehicle, then let his gaze sweep over the black cows in the snowy fields and up the mountainsides to the blue sky above. Being here — in Kings Meadow, on this ranch — made Trevor feel a bit lucky himself. There was a . . . *rightness* about it. Hard to say why he felt that way, but there it was. It was almost like . . . like coming home. Which made no sense whatsoever. He might sing country music and like to ride horses, but he'd grown up in the city. He'd never lived on a ranch or been a John Denver–style country boy. And although he loved his mom, he'd never held great affection for the place where he'd grown up. Too many bad memories were attached to it.

After opening the gate again for Rodney to drive through, he got into the cab for the short trip back to the barn.

"I appreciate your help, Trevor. I want you to know that."

"Would you believe me if I told you I like doing it?"

"Yes, I'd believe you. I've always enjoyed it myself. Too much not to believe you."

Trevor heard the pleasure in the older man's voice. "Penny said all of the cows out there are going to have calves in two or three months. She said they all give birth every year. Is that right?"

"Yes. That's how a ranch like ours operates. We own a couple of bulls, and we also breed by artificial insemination."

"So why aren't there any calves out there

now? You know. The older ones that were born early this year."

Rodney stopped the truck and turned off the engine. "The calves are sold after they're weaned. By the time they're nine or ten months old, usually. By then their mothers are a few months away from giving birth again."

Will I still be here when the births start to happen? As the question drifted through his mind, he realized he hoped the answer would be yes.

CHAPTER 9

Located south of town, Bill and Donna Carter's large, two-story home overlooked the river. The great room stretched across the entire length of the house and had a wall of windows that afforded spectacular views of the rushing water below and the rugged mountains beyond. Penny had attended many social events in the Carter home over the years. Both Bill and Donna loved to entertain, and Tess, their only child, was a natural hostess. Had been from an early age.

"Come in. Come in." Tess's smile was warm. "I'm so glad you came." Behind her, the sound of many voices raised in conversations drifted into the entry hall.

Even though she knew otherwise, Penny said, "I hope I'm not late."

"No. You aren't late. I expect a few more guests, actually. Here." She held out a hand. "Let me take your coat."

Penny obliged and Tess took the coat into

the nearby den. When she returned, she hooked arms with Penny and escorted her down the hall to the great room. It was filled with people who stood in groups of twos and threes or more, talking, laughing. Most had beverages in hand. Some were nibbling on munchies of one kind or another. As Tess had promised, Penny knew everyone she saw. She'd grown up with the majority of them, although some had been several years ahead of her in school and some several years behind her.

The doorbell rang, and Tess released Penny's arm. "Get yourself something to drink." She motioned toward the far side of the room. "I'll be right back." Then she hurried away.

Before Penny could move, Skye and Grant Nichols greeted her. Married for two months, each glowed with newlywed love.

"What do you think?" Skye drew Penny a little deeper into the room. "Will we survive whatever Tess has in store for us tonight?"

Penny laughed softly. "I hope so."

Grant said, "I was on my way to get something to drink for Skye and me. Can I get you anything, Penny?"

"No, thanks. I'm good for now."

Grant walked away, his wife's gaze following him.

"You look so happy." Penny had worried some about her friend's whirlwind courtship. The wedding had taken place less than four months after the couple met. But it appeared her worries had been for nothing.

"I am happy," Skye answered. "Deliriously happy, as a matter of fact. I highly recommend the institution of marriage."

Penny felt a slight twinge of envy. Surprising since she'd never felt an urgent need to find Mr. Right. Someday it would happen. Someday she would meet a man she would love. Someday. At the right time. In the right way. But now was not the right time. Her heart was too broken to make room for anyone to find a home there.

Movement in the entry hall drew Penny's gaze away from Skye. Surprise replaced envy when she saw Tess and Trevor enter the great room, Tess holding his arm the same way she'd held Penny's only minutes before.

"They make a striking couple, don't they?" Skye whispered. "It sure didn't take Tess long to rope in the new guy."

A desire for the quiet of home swept over Penny, but it was too late now. She was here and here she would stay. Deep down, she even knew it was good for her to be among her friends, to do something just for fun.

Still, the desire to leave was strong. She frowned. *And it has nothing to do with Tess's arm in Trevor's.*

Grant returned at that moment with Skye's beverage, a welcome distraction. Penny quickly asked Skye a question about their Hawaiian honeymoon. Her friend was only too willing to answer, and the stories that followed took up enough time for the temptation to leave to subside.

Tess seemed in no hurry to tear herself away from Trevor's side or to begin the game portion of the evening. She introduced him to one group of friends after another, making a slow but steady turn around the room. Thanks to the Christmas bazaar, Sunday's church service, his part-time job, and the previous night's Bible study, Trevor had met many of them, and even those he hadn't. met made him feel welcome.

The circle of introductions was complete when Tess and Trevor stopped before Penny Cartwright and her two friends. Not that Trevor hadn't been aware of her presence. He'd noticed her the instant he'd stepped into the room.

Tess said, "You know Penny, I think. And this is Skye and Grant Nichols." She hugged Trevor's arm a little closer to her side.

"Everybody, this is Trevor Reynolds."

"We met last night." Grant offered his hand.

With a nod, Trevor shook it, then said to Skye, "A pleasure to meet you, Mrs. Nichols."

"Call me Skye." She smiled for a moment, then a look of realization filled her eyes. "Wait. Trevor Reynolds? You're that Nashville singer. Brad was your drummer."

He hadn't tried to hide that fact, but neither had he broadcast it to everyone he'd met in Kings Meadow. And his past had been surprisingly easy to keep to himself from all but a very few people. He'd enjoyed the anonymity more than he'd expected. He'd liked not having to be "on" all the time. Strange, wasn't it? He'd chased fame for such a long time without ever achieving it, at least not at the level he'd dreamed of. And now here he was, sorry when someone actually recognized his name.

"Yes," he answered at last. "That would be me."

Then his gaze shifted to Penny. Although she made a valiant effort not to show it, the mention of Brad and Trevor's band had unsettled her. Or at least he was convinced that was the reason for the tension in her shoulders and the thinning of her lips.

How do we get past this?

Skye intruded on his thoughts. "We would love to hear you sing sometime."

Penny looked brittle enough to break in two.

"Maybe sometime," he answered, his gaze remaining on Penny.

Grant said something before drawing his wife away.

Lowering his voice, Trevor asked Penny, "Would you like me to leave? I don't have to be here."

"Why would she want —" Tess began, then abruptly fell silent.

Penny shook her head. "No. You needn't leave. You're Tess's guest." Her shoulders shuddered slightly as she let out a breath. "And it isn't your fault that I react this way when someone mentions my brother. I . . . I know that."

In that moment, Trevor felt as if he and Penny had taken a giant step forward. Not that she'd forgiven him. Not that she wanted to be friends with him. But they seemed to have made some progress since the last time they were together. At least she wasn't fleeing his presence or wishing he would leave instead.

Still, he wasn't going to press his luck. It was time he stopped invading her space. He glanced at Tess. "I think I'd like that Coke now."

"Of course. The drinks are over here." She smiled, although not as brightly as before, then drew him toward the far wall. After a few steps, she softly said, "That was awkward."

"Sorry."

"Is it only because you remind her of Brad?"

"Mostly." It was a half-truth, but he didn't feel compelled to say Penny held him responsible for what happened to her brother. Tess didn't need to know that. It seemed a private matter.

They stopped at the fancy bar. Tess went to the opposite side and, ignoring the small refrigerator, opened the wheeled cooler that was on the floor. "Regular or diet?"

"Regular. Thanks."

She wiped moisture from the bottle with a small towel, then handed him the beverage. "So it was *your* band. I should have recognized your name, I guess, but I don't remember hearing it before last weekend." As the last words left her mouth, her face turned red.

Trevor surprised them both by laughing. "You're not alone, Tess, if that makes you feel any better. There are more people who have never heard of me than I care to admit."

"So what on earth made you come here? Are you giving up your career?"

"No. Not giving it up. Just taking a break." His gaze swept the room in search of Penny. "I needed some time off after the accident." He saw her, standing near the fireplace.

Tess touched the back of his hand, drawing his eyes back to her. "Were you badly injured in the crash?"

This wasn't a conversation he wanted to have. Not here and now, and not with Tess. He settled for giving a slow shake of his head.

"I guess you came to Kings Meadow to lick your wounds," she said softly. "Just like me after my divorce."

He knew his smile was tight. "I suppose you're right."

She offered a fleeting smile of her own before stepping out from behind the bar and moving toward the wall of windows. Once there, she raised her hands and her voice. "All right, everybody. It's time we got started. Please make your way to one of the tables set up around the room. Once everyone is seated, I'll reveal the game to be played at each table."

Trevor's mother loved to play board

games. She always had. Growing up, he'd been exposed to the latest craze and to classic games and to most everything in between. Chances were good, whatever table he chose, he would have an edge over the other players.

He went to the first table that had an available chair. There were six participants in all. Trevor even remembered the names of the two guys who, in the manner of lifelong friends, joked and laughed to fill the time until their hostess arrived with their board game — Monopoly.

Thanks, Mom. I've got this.

Only it wasn't going to be quite that simple. The rules for this party included a kind of musical chairs. When an alarm went off after an unspecified amount of time, scores would be tallied and participants would then have to move to a different table and a different game, men moving clockwise, women moving counterclockwise. Trevor had a feeling that chaos was about to ensue.

Penny fully expected to hate the evening. She anticipated a blinding headache to develop because of the loud voices and bursts of laughter. But much to her surprise, she was wrong. She found herself invested in whatever game she played, and when she wasn't seriously trying to beat someone, she was laughing as loudly as anyone else. The silliness was contagious. She didn't even mind when she found herself seated opposite Trevor for the final round.

"Five minutes to go over the rules," Tess declared. "Ready? Begin."

The game on their table was called Balderdash. Penny had never heard of it. The same was not true of Trevor. He made that obvious as he took the lead in explaining the rules of the game and scarcely had to look at the instruction card. It was also apparent that he was having a whale of a good time.

That was another surprise for her: the way he fit in with such ease. Most of the people in the room had been friends since grade school, yet he didn't seem like an outsider. Maybe after all his years of moving from place to place to perform, he'd learned how to assimilate. Or maybe his ability to fit in was a performance in itself.

"Wait 'til you hear Trevor sing, Pen," Brad's voice whispered in her memory. *"He's good. He's* real *good."*

Is he really *that good*?

Her brother had given her Trevor's eponymous CD for Christmas last year, but she'd been so angry over his decision to leave

Kings Meadow — and over the part Trevor Reynolds had played in that decision — that she'd never listened to it. Not even to a single track. She supposed the CD was in a drawer in the house. Maybe her dad knew where it was.

"All right," Trevor said, bringing her back to the present. "Here we go." He rolled the dice.

Penny tried to play well, but the ability to concentrate seemed to have vanished for good. When the alarm rang, signaling the end of the final round, Penny's playing piece had been left woefully behind. Scorecards were collected and tallied by Tess, and then the silly dollar-store prize was awarded to none other than Trevor Reynolds. He laughed and accepted it from their hostess as if it were his first Grammy.

The words of profuse thanks were hardly out of his mouth before Tess leaned in and gave him a light peck on the cheek while holding his upper arm with both hands. It was something Penny had seen her do with others, both male and female, through the years. Often. And, for that matter, more than once tonight. It was simply part of her flirty, vivacious nature. What surprised Penny was the flash of embarrassment that swept across Trevor's face. There and then gone. Hardly time for anyone to notice. Anyone except Penny, perhaps, and after a few minutes, even she began to wonder if she'd seen it. After all, he must be used to attractive women hanging on to him wherever he went. Country-star handsome and oozing with charisma and charm. What woman wouldn't be attracted to him?

Even me?

Oh, how she despised that thought. And it wasn't true. She wasn't attracted to him. Not in the least.

Still, despite everything, Penny had to admit Trevor was . . . likable, and his very likability was making it hard to continue hating him, blaming him.

"Excuse me," she whispered to the others at the table. Then she rose and slipped unnoticed from the room, making a hasty departure.

She would have to ask Tess's forgiveness later.

Trevor's telephone started to ring just as he turned the key in the lock of his front door. He tossed his hat onto the sofa on his way to answer it. Given the lateness of the hour, he was sure he knew who would be on the other end.

"Hello."

"Trevor, dear." As suspected, it was his mom. "I was so glad to learn you have a phone again. I hated feeling out of touch."

He shucked out of his coat and dropped it onto the sofa next to his hat. "What's up? Nothing's wrong, is it?"

"No, dear. Nothing's wrong. But I did want to ask if you are certain you won't be home for Christmas. Because if you can come, I want to make plans around your visit."

They'd had this discussion a few times already. "Not this year, Mom. I need to stay put. I'm not sure I understand why myself, but I feel like I *need* to be here. At least for a time."

"I wish I could help," she said, almost too softly to hear. Then, a little louder, "Whatever it is you're going through, I wish I could help."

"You've always been there for me, Mom. Always."

"Not always, Trevor. Not in every way I needed to be. And I'm so sorry."

"Mom —"

"We both know that's true."

He wished he could reach through the phone lines and give her a hug. He knew she blamed herself for not being more of a buffer between him and his father when

158

Trevor had still been a boy. He'd tried to tell her that he understood, that it was all right, that he could deal with the memories, but she couldn't seem to believe him. Maybe because it wasn't entirely true. "I love you, Mom. Do you know that?"

"Yes." She paused a moment. "Yes, of course I know. And I love you."

"How about you and I take a little trip for Mother's Day? Maybe to Catalina Island."

"That would be lovely."

He heard what she didn't say: that Mother's Day was far, far off and she missed him now. Was it possible that he was wrong about where he was supposed to be for Christmas? Maybe it wasn't God who wanted him in Kings Meadow. After all, what did he know about hearing from God?

His mom put on a brave voice. "Well, tell me more about Kings Meadow and what you've been doing since we last talked. Were you out having fun this evening?"

Trevor smiled as he leaned back on the sofa, settling in for a lengthy chat.

BRAD

2009

Kings Meadow usually escaped the worst of summer heat, surrounded as it was by mountains. But this year the month of July had already broken high-temperature records for ten days running. Which was why Brad, his sister — home from college on summer break — and a bunch of their friends were trying to escape the heat at a favorite swimming hole. The oval-shaped pond was fed by a clear, cold-running creek, the water tumbling down out of the mountains, then in turn emptying into the river a quarter mile below.

A few years ago, a rope and tire had been hung from an ancient tree, perfect for swinging over the pond and dropping into the water, hopefully making a big splash that would catch sunbathers unaware. On his turn, Brad planned to aim his spray at Penny and her boyfriend from Boise, Curt Lansing. Neither Penny nor Curt had been

160

swimming yet. Instead, they'd spent all of their time sitting on large beach towels, heads close together — talking, smiling, laughing.

Brad stepped onto the tire with one foot and grabbed hold of the rope between two large knots. Then he pushed off with the other foot, swinging out over the deepest part of the pond. He let go, and as he plummeted toward the water, he grabbed his knees to his chest to form a cannonball. He hit the water just right. He'd done this often enough to know the direction of the spray.

Breaking the surface, he swirled toward Penny. She and Curt were standing now, shaking the water off their hair like wet dogs. Penny caught Brad's gaze, and for a second or two she looked genuinely angry. But then she started to laugh.

Penny never had been able to stay angry with her little brother for long. Brad had figured that out when he was still a kid, and if he was honest, he'd taken advantage of it on more than one occasion. He missed getting to tease her and play practical jokes on her when she was away at college. But maybe that made it all the more fun once she was home for the summer.

He swam to the side of the pond near his sister and pulled himself out of the water onto the ledge, still grinning. "Oops. Sorry, Pen."

"Sure you are. Pest."

He shrugged as he slicked his wet hair back from his face. Penny responded by snapping a towel at him, missing his arm by no more than an inch.

He feigned a glower. "Oh, you would've been in so much trouble, big sister."

She laughed again, dropped the towel, and then dove into the water, swimming with strong arms toward the opposite side. Curt followed right behind.

The guy had it bad for Penny, no two ways about it. But Brad knew his sister wouldn't let things go too far. She wouldn't let herself fall in love until she'd graduated. Maybe not until Brad had graduated from college too.

She'd been after him all summer about deciding what he wanted to do after he finished high school, where he wanted to go to college, what he wanted to study. His best subjects had always been math and science, and Penny thought he should become an engineer of one kind or another. It was a practical career, she said. He could make a good living at it.

He didn't have the heart to tell her he would much rather study music. In fact, if

162

he didn't have to think of anybody but himself, he would skip college altogether and become part of a band — the sooner, the better. But his dad and sister both placed a premium on higher education. He wouldn't do anything to disappoint them if he could help it.

Only someday he was going to follow his dream. Someday he would have to, no matter what.

CHAPTER 10

Penny awakened the next morning feeling grumpy and out of sorts, more tired than when her head hit the pillow. Her dreams had left her unsettled, although in the light of day she couldn't recall the particulars. The illuminated digits of the clock on the nightstand said it was nearly eight o'clock. It was a rare thing that she slept this late, even on her days off. She'd always been an early riser. Even as a toddler, according to her dad.

She sat up and switched on the bedside lamp. Warm air pumped through the floor vent to chase the chill of winter from the room, and the scent of coffee wafted under the door, making it impossible for her to linger any longer under the down comforter. After tossing aside the covers, she reached for her robe at the same time she put her feet into a pair of fluffy slippers. She knotted the belt around her waist as she headed out of the room.

"Dad?" she called when she reached the top of the stairs.

"In the kitchen."

"Sorry I slept in. I hope you waited for me to feed the cows."

Her dad appeared in the kitchen doorway and watched her descent. "No worries. They're already taken care of."

"Dad . . ." She drew out the word in a gentle scold.

"I didn't do it alone. Trevor helped."

She felt her heart skitter. "Trevor was here this morning?"

"Bright and early." Her dad turned back into the kitchen. "I'm about to scramble some eggs. How many do you want?"

"Just one." She stepped through the doorway and stopped.

Her dad stood at the stove, the eggs on the counter to his right, butter beginning to sizzle in the skillet before him. Trevor sat at the breakfast table, holding a mug of coffee while reading the weekly local newspaper. He looked totally at ease, totally at home. Wishing she'd taken a moment to brush her tousled hair, Penny pinched the top of her robe together.

Trevor looked up. "Good morning." His jaw was dark with the stubble of a beard. A good look on him, as it so happened.

"Morning," she mumbled as she headed for the coffee.

"You left awful fast last night. Tess looked all over for you."

"I . . . I had a headache." It wasn't a total fabrication. "I thought it was better to slip out and not disturb the fun."

"Sorry about the headache. It did get loud. But it quieted down after the games were over and people settled down a bit."

Her dad whipped raw eggs in a bowl with a fork. "Sounds like everybody had a good time."

"Turned out to be more fun than I expected," Trevor answered. "I'm glad I went." He met Penny's gaze again. "What about you? Did you have fun, despite the headache?"

"Yes," she said with reluctance, not wanting to admit it to herself, let alone to him. "I did."

Trevor closed the newspaper, folded it in half, then in half again. "I've traveled a lot over the years. Been in a lot of cities and towns. Sometimes for long stretches, mostly for short. But I don't think I've been anywhere that the folks have made me feel as welcome as I've felt here."

With one exception. Guilt pierced her. *Me.*

166

I've done my best to make you feel very unwelcome.

She tried to see that same accusation in his eyes. She wanted him to accuse her of being unfriendly — because it was true. But she couldn't see it. He wasn't accusing her of anything.

Her dad said, "Sit down, Pen. These eggs are just about ready."

Obediently, she carried her mug of coffee to the table and sat opposite Trevor. The table had already been set for three, and she suspected Trevor had had a hand in that too. A minute later her dad set a platter of eggs and another of buttered toast in the middle of the table, followed soon after by a pitcher of orange juice. Her father joined them at the table, and after he said a brief blessing, he handed the platter of eggs to her and the platter of toast to Trevor. No one spoke as they put food on their plates.

Penny reached behind her neck and looped her long hair into a loose knot at the nape to keep it from falling forward as she ate. She tried not to think about her appearance — ancient bathrobe, disheveled hair, and more than likely smudges of the mascara that hadn't been entirely washed away last night before going to bed. It wasn't fair that she should be put at such a disadvantage here in her own kitchen. And Trevor Reynolds sitting there, all comfortable and relaxed and looking totally rested despite remaining at the party longer and getting up earlier to help her dad.

Focusing her eyes on her plate, she ate without tasting the breakfast she chewed and swallowed.

"We're going to put up our Christmas tree and decorations today," her dad said after a lengthy silence. "Care to join us, Trevor? You're more than welcome. Unless you have other plans."

Penny held her breath.

"No other plans. Thanks. It's been years since I helped decorate a tree. I'd like to stay if you're sure I won't be in the way."

She suspected Trevor glanced in her direction when he said the latter, but she refused to look up to see if she was right.

Her dad was quick to reply, "Of course you won't be in the way. The more the merrier. And besides, this is the season when folks are supposed to be drawn together. No one should be alone at Christmas."

It isn't Christmas yet. The thought made her feel petty. *Because it should. I am being petty.*

She rose from her chair. "Thanks for the breakfast, Dad. I'm going to shower and get dressed." Her gaze flicked to Trevor, then down to her empty plate. She picked it up, along with her table service and juice glass, and carried everything to the sink, where she left them before hurrying from the kitchen. She hoped against hope that a hot shower would put her life back into clear perspective once again.

Trevor leaned back in his chair. "I thought I was making some progress with her. I guess not. She really can't stand being around me for long."

"Maybe. Maybe not." Rodney shook his head slowly. "You can't always tell with Penny. Still waters run deep, as they say."

Trevor didn't argue with the older man, but he was convinced he knew better in this instance. Penny blamed him for her brother's death — for becoming his friend, for enticing him away, for hiring him as his drummer, for taking him on the road, for allowing him to drive when he was tired — and she wasn't ever going to forgive him, no matter how hard he tried to change her mind. Too bad, because the truth was he liked her. He couldn't say why. It wasn't as if she'd ever been warm and welcoming around him. But that didn't seem to matter. He was drawn to her anyway.

Rodney pushed his chair back from the table. "I'll do the dishes, and then you and I can get the Christmas boxes from the garage."

"No, sir." Trevor stood. "Not this time. You cooked. I'll clean up. You sit there and enjoy another cup of coffee."

Rodney smiled. "If you insist." Then he chuckled again. "I'm nobody's fool."

Trevor cleared the table in no time. After scraping food off the dishes into the trash can, he added dish soap to the sink before filling it with hot water.

"Good of you to do that for me," Rodney said. "But we do have a dishwasher." He pointed at the appliance.

"I've never minded washing dishes. Good thing since I live alone when I'm not on the road."

"What was Brad's place like in Nashville?"

"It was a big old house that one of the other band members inherited from his grandparents. Three of the guys in the band lived there, along with a couple of other roommates."

Rodney was silent for a short while, then, softly, he said, "Wish I'd taken a trip down there to see it and meet all of the band and get to know Nashville. He really loved it there." Another silence. "It would have been nice to have some memories of him there, I think."

Trevor felt the older man's pain as if it were his own, and his throat tightened with emotion.

Brad's dad continued, "It's not right, you know, your child dying first. It's every parent's worst nightmare."

Trevor turned, wiping his hands on a dish towel. "I'm sure that's true."

"When a parent dies, there is pain and loss, but at least there's a natural order to it. Losing a child . . ." Rodney's voice drifted into silence as he shook his head.

"I wish I could change it, sir."

"I know, my boy. I know. But you can't. No one can. So I simply ask God for an extra portion of His grace to see me through each day."

Trevor turned back to the sink, moistened a dishcloth, and then finished wiping the countertop. When he turned a second time, he found the older man rising from his chair, only a trace of melancholy remaining in his expression.

"Let's get those decorations moved into the house," he said.

"I'm ready." Trevor tossed the damp dish towel onto the counter.

It was soon apparent that the Cartwright family didn't do Christmas in a small way. There were six large plastic storage bins to be carried into the house, each of them filled to capacity with decorations.

"The tree's outside next to the garage," Rodney said after the last bin had been brought inside. "We can —"

"I'll get it." Trevor didn't bother to put on his coat. He wouldn't be outside all that long. He exited the house through the mudroom and made his way to the far side of the garage. Tall and thick, the tree lay on top of a pile of shoveled snow. Trevor could see that it would fill the corner in the living room where Rodney had indicated it would go.

He managed to carry the tree into the house without too much trouble, and together he and Rodney secured it into the tree stand. Then they stepped back to admire their handiwork.

"Beautiful tree," Rodney said. "Even without ornaments. Our friends got it for us when they went to chop down their own tree."

"This one isn't from the lot in town, huh?"

Rodney shook his head. "When the kids were little, my wife and I always made a day of it for the family. Going into the forest in search of the perfect tree. Coming back home and drinking hot chocolate while we decorated it. Those were such good times."

Trevor felt a sting of envy. His childhood memories were mostly of arguments, angry words, and slamming doors. Not that his mom hadn't tried her best to make the season bright, but his father —

"This year," Rodney continued, "well, this year neither Penny nor I had the energy to do it that way, but it still wouldn't have felt right to buy one off the lot. So we were thankful when Tom and Janet volunteered to get a tree for us while they were getting theirs."

Trevor's father had never had much in the way of Christmas spirit. William Reynolds had been more of the bah-humbug type. He'd complained about the crass commercialization of the holiday, but he just hadn't liked to shop for gifts. As for decorating a Christmas tree — they'd had an artificial one — the man had never hung so much as one ornament on a single branch in all of the years Trevor was at home.

"Ah, here's Penny," Rodney said, intruding once again on Trevor's wandering thoughts. "Now we can get started."

Penny walked to her father and gave him a quick kiss on the cheek before looking at the tree in the corner. "It's a beautiful tree, Dad."

"That's what I said. Wasn't it, Trevor?"

"Yes, sir. It was."

Rodney walked over to the entertainment center and fiddled with a few controls. Moments later, soft Christmas music came through speakers in opposite corners of the room.

"Hot chocolate now or wait awhile?" Penny asked.

Her dad answered, "Let's wait."

In unison, father and daughter popped lids off two of the bins. Trevor grinned as he watched them pull out strings of lights and all manner of other festive decorations. His mother would have called them *doodads* and *whatnots,* and she had a great fondness for the same, especially during the Christmas season. Where his dad had been a bah-humbug type, Dorothy Reynolds — her friends called her Dot — was of the deck-the-halls variety.

But she had nothing on the Cartwrights.

"What are you smiling about?" Rodney asked.

Trevor gave his head a slow shake, then

answered, "My mom. She would love this." A wave of his arm took in the tree and all of the bins.

Rodney stood a little straighter, his eyes widening. "Well, why not ask her to come to Kings Meadow for the holidays? You're staying in town, you said, so why not have her join you?"

"There wouldn't be much room for her in my little apartment. She'd likely go stir-crazy, especially when I was at work. I don't even have a television to occupy her time."

"Then she could stay with us." Rodney looked toward Penny and back again. "We've got extra bedrooms, and she'd be more than welcome."

Trevor shook his head again, even though the offer was tempting. More than tempting. His mom had sounded disappointed when they talked last night. Maybe she wouldn't come, but it might help her to be asked. "That's really nice of you, sir, but —"

"We insist. Don't we, Penny? You and your mother shouldn't be apart for Christmas."

"She'll probably decline." As the words left his mouth, he doubted they were true.

"Ask her anyway. And if she comes, she can make her visit as long as she likes. You

175

can show her a bit of Idaho while she's here."

His mom and snow. Would she enjoy being surrounded by so much white? Probably not for an extended period. His mom preferred the beach and soft, warm breezes. But she'd be okay for a few days or even a week.

"I imagine it's too early in California to call now," Rodney pressed, "but do it as soon as you think you can. She'll have to make her flight reservations right away. Use our phone. We've got an unlimited long-distance plan."

Trevor could see there was no point in arguing with Rodney Cartwright. He would call his mom and see what she said to the invitation.

Penny spent the good portion of the next hour wrestling with her feelings even as she worked side by side with her dad and Trevor. It was her opinion that her dad shouldn't have invited Trevor's mother to come stay with them. The woman was a complete stranger. And besides, it would cause her dad extra work — work that he didn't need added to his days. Not to mention that if the woman stayed at the ranch, Trevor would be there even more hours

176

than he was now.

Maybe she should have said something at the first mention of Mrs. Reynolds coming to stay over Christmas, but she'd swallowed the words, determined not to provide more evidence of her unfriendly nature. Her dad had always been Mr. Hospitality. Like Brad, their dad had a gift for welcoming people into his life. A gift Penny hadn't inherited, that was for certain.

At ten o'clock, with the living room, entry hall, and banister all decorated, Trevor excused himself and went to make the phone call to his mother.

"Pray that she'll agree to come," her dad whispered as soon as Trevor was out of sight.

"Dad, wouldn't it be better if —"

"This is important, Penny. My heart tells me she's supposed to be here. Maybe Trevor needs to be with her more than he lets on."

She pressed her lips together, swallowing further objections.

"Pen. Do it for me."

"All right, Dad." *But I still don't think it's a good idea.*

She prayed silently, as asked, but it was halfhearted at best. And if God had to choose between her prayer and her father's, she knew whose prayer would get answered. At least she didn't have to wait long. In less than ten minutes Trevor returned to the living room, wearing a soft smile.

"Well?" her dad asked, as if the answer wasn't obvious.

Trevor raked the fingers of one hand through his hair. "She said she'd love to come."

"Wonderful. How soon can we expect her?"

"She'll check flights right away. If there's a seat available, she'll probably come next weekend."

Her dad beamed with undeniable pleasure.

If it makes him that happy, I shouldn't begrudge him. I won't begrudge him. So help me, I won't. I will welcome Mrs. Reynolds — and her son — into this home . . . even if it kills me.

That evening, Trevor sat on the sofa in his apartment, the only light in the room coming from above the stove. The hours he'd spent at the Cartwright ranch had been filled with good spirits and laughter. He'd felt a part of something he'd never been part of before. By comparison, his apartment was empty and silent.

He reached for his guitar. After a few moments, he strummed a few chords. Song

178

titles drifted through his head, popular songs that he'd covered through the years, but none of them enticed him to play and sing the way they should have, the way they used to. Nothing until the title of his mom's favorite hymn came to him. With barely a conscious thought, he changed chords and began to softly sing, "Amazing grace! How sweet the sound that saved a wretch like me! I once was lost, but now am found; was blind, but now I see."

A kind of hunger swelled in his heart in response to the words. Words he'd heard many times before. Words he'd memorized. And yet they felt new. Alive with a meaning he hadn't understood before.

" 'Twas grace that taught my heart to fear, and grace my fears relieved; how precious did that grace appear the hour I first believed."

He remembered Brad, the way the young man's faith had seemed to shine through him, like sunlight through a stained-glass window. Emotions choked his throat. His fingers lowered from the strings of the guitar, plunging the room into silence.

"God," he whispered, "I want a faith like Brad's. I don't want to be the guy I've been for so long. I'm trying to straighten out my life, but I don't think I can do it on my own.

I want what You want for me. Not just a taste of it. Not just until I like myself better. Help me."

The apartment was still as dark as it had been minutes ago. It was still silent. But now it didn't feel as empty. He didn't feel so alone.

He was a novice at this kind of stuff, but he believed he'd just received an answer to prayer.

BRAD
2010

"You're the fourth caller. Can you name the artist and the year the song hit number one?"

Brad's heart was beating so loud in his chest he could hardly hear himself think. "Brooks and Dunn. And the year was . . . 2005."

"That's right. We've got a winner. Hold on, young man, and we'll get some more information from you."

While music played through the telephone, Brad stared at his best friend, Charlie Regal. *I won,* he mouthed in disbelief.

He'd never won anything before in his life. Not anything like this, anyway. Tickets for four to a three-day outdoor country music festival to be held that coming summer in Utah. Meeting the artists, T-shirts, and more.

When Brad was finally off the phone, he and Charlie raced up the stairs to the laptop computer in his bedroom. In no time at all, he pulled up the website for the music festival and scrolled through the list of artists. There were a couple of major names among them. The others he would have to check out.

"Can you believe it, Charlie? We're gonna get to see these guys in person. We're gonna get to meet them."

"We?"

"Are you kidding?" He punched his friend in the arm. "Of course you're going with me. You and two others."

"Your dad and Penny."

Brad shrugged. "I don't know. It isn't Dad's kind of thing. And besides, he'll say he hates to ask someone to take care of the livestock while he's away for several days. Penny might be interested. She likes country music. I'm just not sure she would want three days and nights of it."

"You think our folks will let just four of us guys go? You know, without a parent along."

"Sure. Why not? We're seventeen. I'll almost be eighteen. We'll all be seniors."

"You know my mom," Charlie said with a shake of his head.

Yeah, Brad knew Mrs. Regal. She'd always been on the overprotective side. Charlie griped about it often, and Brad thought he had good reason to complain. His own dad was strict, but he gave Brad freedom. Enough freedom even to make mistakes he could learn from.

He laid a hand on Charlie's shoulder. "We'll ask a couple of older friends then. And we've got four months to work on her. By the time of the festival, she'll be glad to have you out of her hair."

They laughed and then both turned their eyes back to the laptop screen.

August was never going to get here fast enough.

CHAPTER 11

Between going to the Cartwright ranch once or twice every day to help feed the cattle, working part time, going to church on Sunday and again for the men's Bible study on Thursday, plus twice meeting Tess Carter — at her invitation — at The Friendly Bean, a quaint little coffee shop a half block away from Main Street, the next week seemed to fly by. Before he knew it, it was time for him to drive down to Boise to meet his mom at the airport.

Trevor had last seen her in early October. After his trip to Kings Meadow for Brad's funeral — ill-fated as that had been — Trevor had returned to his boyhood home in California for a couple of weeks. The visit had been good for them both. He'd needed to be away from Nashville, his bandmates, and all reminders of the young man who had lost his life. His mom had needed reassurance that he was okay, that the injuries he'd sustained in the accident were minor and mending.

Even so, it had surprised Trevor how quickly his mom accepted the invitation to come to Idaho for Christmas. Belatedly, he'd realized she wasn't as all right with him not coming home for Christmas as she'd tried to make him believe. It shamed him. He should have known her real feelings, even if she'd hidden them from him.

He couldn't have asked for a better day for her to see Idaho for the first time. The sky was cloudless, a crystal-blue expanse, sunlight glinting off the snowy landscape. The highway was clear and dry, no ice or snowpack to make his mom nervous on the return trip. The temperature in Kings Meadow was supposed to hit forty by mid-afternoon. Still too cold for his mom, but better than it might have been and still could be before her visit was over.

He drove to the airport without any trouble, thanks to a somewhat foggy memory from his trip in September and to the GPS on his phone. He appreciated the latter the most. It was nice to have cellular service again, even if it was only for a few hours.

At the airport he parked his truck, checked his watch, and headed into the terminal to

185

await his mom. Inside, he looked at the arrival board. His mom's plane was on time. Maybe ten minutes until it was scheduled to land. He took a seat in the waiting area outside the security exit and amused himself with people watching.

There was a young mother with two little boys, the oldest perhaps four, struggling to keep both of them nearby when what they wanted most was to run and squeal. Trevor felt her exhaustion from twenty feet away.

There was a group of teenagers, a mix of boys and girls, all of them holding signs, welcoming home someone named Jacob.

There was a middle-aged man in a business suit, seated in the same row of chairs as Trevor, who never looked up from his phone as he answered e-mails or texts or both, one right after another.

There were a couple of tall, beanpole-thin cowboys — brothers by the look of them — complete with tight jeans, dusty boots, and well-worn hats. One of them had a handlebar mustache, perhaps trying to look older than he was. Trevor wouldn't have been surprised if they had horses tied up outside the terminal. He grinned at the thought.

A flood of passengers started to come through the automatic doors. Trevor rose from the chair and checked the arrival board again. According to it, his mom's plane hadn't landed yet, so he resumed his seat and watched as the cowboys welcomed an elderly woman whom he guessed to be their grandmother. The joy on all of their faces caused Trevor to smile again. Then an eruption of voices drew his eyes to a soldier in fatigues whose name was obviously Jacob. The girls in his welcoming committee were grinning and crying at the same time.

There was a lull in exiting passengers, and then another steady stream began. This time the arrival board told Trevor that his mother's plane had landed. In expectation, he stepped out of the waiting area where he could more easily see and be seen. He didn't have long to wait. Over the heads of others he recognized his mom's dark brown hair that she'd worn in the same style from as far back as he could remember. He raised his arm and waved to get her attention. A minute later he held her in a warm embrace.

"Glad you came, Mom."

"I'm glad you asked." She laid the fingertips of one hand on his cheek and stared into his eyes. "You look good."

"Feel good too." He took the small carry-on bag from her hand. "Come on. Let's get your suitcase."

They took the escalator to the ground

level and made their way to the luggage carousels. After finding the correct one for his mother's airline, they joined the other passengers gathered around it.

"Did you bring a warm coat?" Trevor asked. "Something more than that sweater you've got on."

"I have a jacket in my carry-on."

"You're going to need more than that. It'll likely get below zero while you're here. We'd better stop at a store and get you something before we leave Boise."

His mom smiled. "Whatever you think's best."

A light on the carousel started to flash and an alarm sounded. Then the machinery started to move. Moments later, the first bag came into view.

"What am I looking for?" Trevor asked.

"A red hard-side suitcase with yellow ribbons on the handles. A large one. You can't miss it."

While they watched and waited, his mother chatted about people he knew from the old neighborhood, ending after several minutes with, "Mrs. Thurgood finally got her new hip last week. And did I tell you Mort Levine got married again?"

"No. You're kidding. Isn't Mr. Levine about a hundred years old?"

She elbowed him in the ribs. "Watch it, you. Mort's only five years older than me." Then she pointed toward the carousel. "There it is. That's mine."

She'd been right. He couldn't have missed it. It was a blaze of color in a sea of black bags. It made him grin and remember all over again why he loved her so much.

Penny put the last of the dishes into the dishwasher, added soap to the dispenser, and started the wash cycle. A glance at the kitchen clock told her that Trevor and his mom should arrive soon.

Anxiety — despite not having any reason to be anxious — tightened her belly. It had been like that ever since she'd known they were to have Trevor's mom as a guest for ten days. Ten days! It meant Trevor would be at the ranch even more often than usual. Plus it seemed like an interminably long time to be saddled with a complete stranger.

Doesn't the Bible have something to say about making strangers welcome? She winced at the thought. *I'm sorry. I don't want an inhospitable nature. God, can You change that?*

Her dad was the definition of hospitable. "This is going to be a good thing, Penny," he'd said more than once over the last week.

"You'll see."

Well, there was no disputing that last part. She would *see* whether or not it was a good thing because there was no escaping it now.

"Penny," her dad called from the living room. "They're here." By the time she reached the entry hall, her dad already had on his coat and was putting on his hat. "Hurry up, slowpoke." He grinned as he reached for the doorknob.

When Penny stepped outside moments later, she saw Trevor rounding the front of his truck to open the passenger door. After helping his mother to the ground, he held on to the crook of her arm while escorting her through the hard-packed snow to the steps and up to the porch.

"Mr. Cartwright. Penny. I'd like you to meet my mom, Dorothy Reynolds."

"Call me Rodney," her dad said as he held out a hand in welcome.

"And I'm Dot. It's so gracious of you to open your home to me."

"Not at all. Not at all. We are glad to do it. Aren't we, Pen?"

"Yes. Of course." As she spoke, she realized the words held some truth. Had her prayer been answered so quickly? "Let's go inside out of the cold before we all freeze to death."

Dot laughed as she clasped the collar of her coat. "It is a bit colder here than at home."

The woman had a lovely laugh and a beautiful smile. It was easy to see where Trevor got both his good looks and his charm.

"Go on in, Mom. I'll get your bags."

Once inside, Penny took Dot Reynolds upstairs to show her the guest room and adjoining bathroom. Before Dot was through saying how lovely everything was, Trevor arrived with her luggage.

Penny stepped toward the door. "Take as long as you like to settle in, Dot. Then come downstairs and I'll give you a tour of the rest of the house."

"See you downstairs, Mom." Trevor followed Penny out of the bedroom. Halfway down the stairs, he said, "I was hoping we'd get back before the midday feeding."

"You did."

"Good."

Pausing at the bottom of the stairs, she faced him. He'd been generous with his time from the start. Except for the hours he worked and slept, he was at the ranch more than anywhere. And because of it, she thought her dad was less tired and in less pain than she'd seen him in months. She was grateful for that.

Why didn't she also admit that Trevor Reynolds wasn't the bad, reckless, horrid, selfish so-and-so she'd made of him in her mind, both before and after her brother's death? Why didn't she admit that he was kind and thoughtful around her, even when she was thoroughly disagreeable? Why didn't she admit that she was beginning to like him?

Like him?

"I'll go feed the cows now," he said. "Care to come along?"

She didn't answer. *Do I like him?*

"Penny?" His eyes seemed to look beyond her expression and right into her heart.

She turned away, lest he see her feelings. Feelings that she couldn't yet reconcile. "Okay. That's a good idea. Let's get them fed." She went to the entrance of the living room. "Dad, Trevor and I are going to feed the stock. I told Mrs. Reynolds to take her time settling in. Not sure how long it will be until she comes down."

Her dad nodded in response. "No worries. I'll just wait here until she does."

A short while later, bundled against the cold, Penny and Trevor headed for the far side of the barn, where they loaded bales of hay onto the flatbed truck. They worked in silence, but it was a comfortable one. She expected to be surprised by that realization, but was surprised instead because she *wasn't* surprised. She smiled at the silliness of that thought.

After completing the feeding, Penny drove the truck back to its covered parking area beside the barn. When she got out of the cab, she heard Harmony's nicker and looked toward the pasture where they kept their horses. The mare bobbed her head and nickered again.

"I haven't got anything for you," Penny called to the horse as she walked in that direction.

Two more horses strode through the packed snow toward the fence and an anticipated treat of some kind.

"I should have brought carrots." Penny stroked Harmony's head. "Sorry about that. Next time."

"I could go get some if you want me to," Trevor offered from a few feet behind her.

She glanced over her shoulder. "No. It's okay. They'll survive."

"Every time I come out here, I think how nice it would be to own a horse again. I may have to give in to it when the snow starts to melt."

Her heart fluttered, an oddly disturbing

sensation. "You're planning to stay that long?"

He closed the distance to stand at the fence, not far from her. "Would you mind so much if I did stay?"

He'd misunderstood her question. She hadn't meant she would mind if he stayed long enough to buy a horse, to still be here when the snow was gone. But was it any wonder he'd misunderstood, after the way she'd treated him so much of the time? But trying to explain, even trying to understand her own feelings, seemed beyond her ability at the moment. Finally, she shrugged, then turned and, holding the mare's muzzle between her hands, pressed her forehead to Harmony's forehead.

Trevor stood there, watching Penny and her horse. He'd love to be an artist or a photographer. He'd love to capture with paint or with film what he saw in Penny's expression right now — her vulnerability, her huge capacity to love.

When Trevor had first arrived in Kings Meadow, his feelings for Penny had been heavily influenced by the stories Brad had told about his sister. But over the past three weeks he'd learned to see her with his own eyes. And he realized now how very much he'd like her to be able to see him the same way, to know and understand him. Could that ever happen? Or would Brad's death always be a barrier between them?

Penny patted the mare's neck again before drawing back. "We'd better go inside. We don't want your mother to feel like you've abandoned her."

"Your dad would never let that happen."

"You're right." She smiled tenderly. "He wouldn't."

They turned in unison and started toward the house.

Sticking his fingertips into the back pockets of his jeans, Trevor cleared his throat. "You know, it might help to know what the plans are while Mom's here. I never have gotten much of an answer from your dad."

"It's simple, Trevor. Dad expects you both — you and your mom — to be part of our Christmas. *All* of our Christmas. That doesn't mean just Christmas Eve or Christmas morning. It means everything. Going caroling. Enjoying the annual sleigh ride. Taking communion at church on Christmas Eve, followed by classic Christmas movies at home. Opening gifts on Christmas morning and then dinner with family and friends. Everything."

"Wow. I should have realized. I never

meant to impose. I thought —"

Penny stopped walking, at the same time touching his arm so that he stopped too. "Don't misunderstand me, Trevor. Dad is happier than I've seen him since . . . since Brad died. He's loved preparing for your mom's visit. Thinking of ways to entertain her. And you. We weren't going to have Christmas dinner at our house this year, but now we are. And you two aren't our only guests. Dad's invited others to join us. I can see how much pleasure that's brought him, too, planning it all." She tipped her head to one side as she looked up at him. Her expression was sad and yet not sad. "I've been trying so hard to protect him from any more pain. Both physical and emotional. Perhaps I went overboard."

He refrained from shaking his head, sensing that she was working things through in her mind and didn't need his agreement or argument.

A slight smile curved the corners of her mouth. "No. Not *perhaps*. I *have* gone overboard. Dad's told me so more than once. I just haven't wanted to believe him." Her smile broadened a little. "I'm really glad you and your mom will be celebrating Christmas with us."

Her last words could have been little more

than politeness, if not for the smile that included him. Something had changed between them today. Without fanfare. Without a lengthy conversation. Without any effort. They had turned a corner for the better. For real this time. What that meant for tomorrow, he couldn't be sure, but he was learning to trust God to take care of the future.

Penny tipped her head toward the house. "Come on. Let's go find out what's next on the agenda."

Caroling . . . sleigh ride . . . communion . . . Trevor had never looked forward to Christmas until now. Mostly because Penny Cartwright would be a part of it all.

CHAPTER 12

Every year, in the days leading up to Christmas, Rodney looked forward to caroling with other members of the Kings Meadow Methodist Church. And although he never would have pressured their houseguest to participate, he was delighted when Dot Reynolds agreed to join him and the others for this year's Monday evening event.

As the carolers congregated in the fellowship hall of the Methodist church, Rodney escorted Dot from one small cluster of people to another, making introductions. More than one person made a point of saying how much they liked her son, and each time it happened her face glowed with a mother's pride. In his opinion, she had cause to be proud of Trevor, if for no other reason than his generous spirit.

Glancing across the fellowship hall to where Trevor stood talking with a few others, Rodney said a quick prayer of thanks for the young man. He hadn't realized what a difference it would make in how he felt, having the extra help that Trevor now provided daily. Help that Penny couldn't always give. Or maybe he'd realized it and simply refused to accept it. Even he had to admit that stubbornness was one of his less admirable qualities. His orthopedist had suggested it might be time to give up ranching altogether. Either that or hire full-time help so that Rodney didn't have to do any of the heavy manual labor that a cow-calf operation required. But he couldn't bear the thought of the first and couldn't afford the second. Not as things were right now.

As he looked in Trevor's direction, Rodney saw Penny enter through a nearby doorway. This was one of two nights a week that she worked until the library closed. He was glad she'd been able to get away in time to join in the fun.

The thought of Penny having fun this Christmas season was another reason to be thankful. Only a few short weeks ago, he wouldn't have thought that possible, despite her efforts to hide the truth from him. But he'd witnessed something ease inside of her in recent days. An answer to prayer.

Penny found him with her gaze, smiled, and waved. Then she started across the room in Rodney's direction.

At the same moment, the choir director, Hillary Mitchell — a statuesque woman in her early fifties with a no-nonsense attitude and, as everyone knew, perfect pitch — appeared on the small stage at the far end of the hall. "All right, everyone. Settle down. Settle down." She motioned downward with the palms of both hands. When conversations finally ceased, she said, "We'll be under way in about fifteen minutes. When the time comes, you will receive a flyer on your way out with all of the songs we will be singing tonight and the order in which they will be sung. Our route will be unchanged from the last few years. If you are new to us, don't worry. Just stick with the crowd. There will be coffee and hot chocolate awaiting us when we return."

Penny reached Rodney's side and slipped her arm through his. "I made it just in time. This is going to be fun."

Her comment confirmed his earlier thoughts, and that caused more thanksgiving to well up in his heart. *"Blessed be the God and Father of our Lord Jesus Christ,"* he quoted silently, *"the Father of mercies and God of all comfort, who comforts us in all our affliction."* Amen.

"Didn't Trevor come?" she asked, her gaze

200

shifting from him to Dot and back again.

Perhaps that question revealed the biggest change of all, Rodney thought as he held back a smile.

Dot answered, "He's here somewhere. Talking to friends."

Tess's gaze swept around the small group standing in a corner of the fellowship hall. "Why don't you all plan to come back to my parents' house when the caroling is over?" Her eyes settled on Trevor and seemed to hold a special invitation just for him.

It wasn't as if he hadn't known from the day they first met that she was interested in him. He'd even enjoyed her company when they'd been together. It had been easy to go along whenever she'd invited him. But this time? It felt all wrong.

"Trevor?" She slipped her arm through his. "What do you think?"

"I don't know. I —"

She leaned a little closer and lowered her voice. "You can't say no."

In that moment, he knew she wanted more than he could give in return. It wasn't the right time or place. *And she's not the right girl.* He looked away, over the heads of the crowd, looking —

"Trevor?"

"Sorry, Tess." As gently as possible, he removed his arm from her grasp. "I'll be going back to the Cartwright ranch with my mom when this is over."

Disappointment flittered across her face, and he was sorry to be the cause. It had been unfair of him to accept her other invitations. Not so much the game night party, with so many in attendance, but definitely meeting her for coffee at The Friendly Bean the previous week. Not once but twice.

Truth was he'd always been reckless with the feelings of others. Especially the women he'd known. But he was changing. God was changing him. And he was going to have to be honest with Tess. He was going to have to let her know that he wasn't interested in anything more than a casual friendship. No dates. No future plans. At least not with her.

He glanced across the fellowship hall again.

"If you're looking for Penny —" Tess pointed. "She's over there with her dad."

Surprised, his gaze flew back to Tess. Had he been looking for Penny?

With a slight tip of her head, Tess gave him a knowing look. A look that said she understood something he hadn't discovered yet.

Penny Cartwright? No. He wasn't interested in her. Not in that way.

Was he?

Hillary Mitchell returned to the stage and announced it was time to get started. Everyone began filing out of the fellowship hall, but before Penny, her dad, and Dot Reynolds had taken more than a few steps, Trevor arrived to take his place next to his mom.

And Penny couldn't help it — she felt a leap of pleasure at the sight of him. At the sight of him alone. She hated to admit it, but when she'd seen him talking to Tess, she'd been afraid Tess would join them. And, if she was honest with herself, she hadn't wanted that.

She frowned, bothered by her awareness of Tess's attraction to Trevor. It wasn't as if it was a new awareness. It had been obvious ever since the day Tess first saw him at the bazaar in this very same hall.

Her dad leaned close. "Is something troubling you?"

She gave her head a small shake, hoping to chase away her thoughts even as she answered, "No. Nothing." She forced a smile as she looked up at him. "It's a beautiful night for caroling."

"That's what I thought when Dot and I drove into town."

"What did the two of you do all day?"

"Not much. She and I sat and visited over coffee for a long time this morning. Trevor came over after getting off work at noon. When he and I were done feeding, he took his mom into town to do some shopping. And the three of us had a quick bite of supper before coming to the church. Did you have time to eat something?"

She nodded, not bothering to tell him it was the other half of the sandwich she'd had for lunch.

Outside, the inky night sky sparkled with stars, like diamonds on a jeweler's velvet display cloth. The air was cold, and snow crunched beneath their feet as they made their way to Main Street. The instant Hillary Mitchell, walking at the front of the procession, saw the first Christmas shoppers, she stopped. In moments, the group had formed a half circle, three rows deep, and begun to sing "Joy to the World!"

Penny felt a twinge of sorrow, remembering that last Christmas Brad had stood between her and their father as they'd sung this same song in this same location. But then her thoughts were pulled to the present by a voice she hadn't heard before. A male voice, not overly loud but strong. Rich timbre. Smooth, with just a hint of a Western twang. She guessed who it was, of course, but turned her head to confirm it. Yes, it was Trevor, and she found herself leaning ever so slightly toward him, trying to hear even better. She envisioned her brother, his arm around her shoulders, whispering in her ear, *"See, didn't I tell you he's great?"* Tears welled in her eyes. Her throat closed, stopping the words of the song from escaping. Thankful for the darkness, she tugged on her knit hat, pulling it lower on her forehead.

As the last strains of the carol drifted upward on the cold night air, Trevor looked in her direction. When their gazes met, he smiled at her. But then he must have seen her sorrow, perhaps even guessed why it was there. His smile faded. She was sorry to see it go. Sorry to be the cause of it going.

Their audience applauded, and Hillary motioned for the band of carolers to follow her farther down the street, looking for more shoppers to serenade. All around Penny, her friends and neighbors talked with one another, their voices merry, befitting the evening and the season. Her heart lifted a little.

"Are you okay?" Trevor asked.

She wasn't sure how it had happened, but Dot and her father were now walking side by side and Trevor was next to her.

"Penny?"

"I'm fine. I was just . . . just . . ." Her words trailed away.

"Thinking of Brad," he finished for her, barely loud enough for her to hear.

She nodded.

"He told me about this tradition."

"He did?" It seemed an odd thing for two guys to talk about.

"Yeah. When you're in a band that tours, there's lots of downtime, lots of hours in a car or a bus or a van. Talking helps stave off boredom. Brad liked to talk about Kings Meadow and his family."

She knew that already, but still she said, "He did?"

"He did. I felt like I knew you and your dad long before I got to meet you."

She drew in a shuddery breath. "I was so angry at him when he left."

"Yeah."

"I said things I shouldn't have said."

"He didn't blame you, Penny. He understood why you were upset. Really, he did."

"Don't be an idiot, Brad. You're throwing

206

your life away. All that schooling. All that money to pay for your education."

"I have to do it. It's what I'm supposed to do, Penny."

"You spoiled, selfish . . . selfish . . ." She'd floundered for the perfect word to call him, and when it came, it was one that would have gotten her behind tanned if her dad had heard.

Brad had stared at her in stunned silence for a long while, and when he spoke at last, all he said was her name. *"Pen."*

"You're never going to amount to anything. Not anything."

She heard the slamming door to her bedroom as clearly now as the day she'd screamed those words. "I was so hateful to him. I wish I could tell him I'm sorry. All of those months . . . I never told him I was sorry."

"He knew. He loved you."

Silent tears tracked down her cheeks. Tears that she'd worked so hard to keep in check. There was no stopping them now.

"Come on." Trevor took her by the arm and gently led her through the group of carolers, not stopping until they were away from lampposts wrapped with twinkling Christmas lights and bright storefronts that invited shoppers to come in from the cold.

207

Not stopping until they were alone in their own little patch of darkness. "It's okay to cry, you know."

He couldn't have known how wrong he was. It wasn't okay to cry, because there was a reservoir full of unshed tears just waiting for the dam to burst. A sob escaped her, then another. She covered her face with her mittens and sobbed again. And again. And again.

Slowly, tenderly, he wrapped her in his arms, her hands and face pressed against his chest. She hadn't the strength to resist, even if she'd wanted to. His kindness no longer surprised her. He patted her back with one hand and murmured soothing sounds near her ear. There was no reason she should be comforted — and yet she was. The broken sobs began to subside, although the tears continued to flow for a while.

Trevor would have done or said just about anything to help ease the pain he'd heard as Penny cried in the cold darkness. Her sobs had made him feel helpless. Holding her, letting her cry against him, had been an instinct, but now that he held her, he didn't want to let go.

This feels right. He looked up at the sky, stars twinkling overhead. *But the timing couldn't be worse.*

He was only beginning to figure out a few things about himself and his life and his ambition and his envy and his pride. He was just starting to understand this new relationship he had with God. He had so much more to learn. And one thing he knew for sure. A romantic relationship wasn't a good idea for now. Not with Tess Carter and definitely not with Penny Cartwright. He could care about Penny because she was Brad's sister. He could love her like he would love a sister of his own if he had one. But he couldn't feel anything more than that. That wasn't why he'd come to Kings Meadow. That wasn't why God had brought him here. He was convinced of that.

Penny had grown still in his arms, and he realized she'd stopped crying. He took a short step back, needing some space between them. "You okay now?" His voice sounded cold and unfeeling in his own ears.

He could barely see her face in the darkness, but he thought she blinked before answering, "Yes. Yes, I'm okay now. I . . . I'm sorry I lost control. We'd better get back to the others before we're missed."

She turned and walked swiftly in the direction of the carolers, never looking back. Trevor wanted to catch up with her. He wanted to apologize, to take her back in his arms. Instead he waited a few heartbeats before he followed. At the back of the group, Penny slipped through an opening to rejoin her father. Trevor chose a different path to get to his mother's side.

His mom looked up, a question in her eyes. He shook his head and pretended that some of the magic hadn't gone out of the night.

BRAD

2010

Trevor Reynolds was the midafternoon performer on the last day of the festival. Brad had never heard of him before, but he liked what he saw and heard. Liked it a lot.

What he liked even more was getting to meet the singer. Unlike the other performers before him, Trevor didn't act rushed or disinterested when Brad was introduced backstage. He met Brad's eyes with a direct gaze and invited him to sit down so they could talk awhile. It wasn't long before Brad shared — in a halting voice — his private dream of being a drummer in a professional band one day.

"How old are you?" Trevor asked once Brad fell silent.

"Seventeen."

"Still in high school?"

Brad nodded. "I'm a senior this fall."

"Are you in a band now?"

"Only the school band."

Trevor smiled. "Nothing wrong with a school band. That gives you a different kind of experience, and all experience is good."

"Yeah, but I can't wait to graduate so I can become a part of something more than that. My dad and sister are all set on me going to college, but I'd —"

"Kid, can I give you a piece of advice?"

"Sure," he answered with enthusiasm. "I'd love some."

"Don't skip college. You'll regret it if you do. I speak from experience." The singer wasn't smiling any longer. His expression said he was dead serious.

But Brad was convinced Trevor was wrong. What difference would college make to a drummer in a country band?

Trevor leaned back in his chair and folded his arms over his chest. His eyes narrowed thoughtfully. "Tell you what," he said after a lengthy silence. "You wait to chase your dream until you graduate from college. If you do that, I'll make sure you get some auditions in Nashville. If I'm in need of a drummer when that time rolls around, I'll even audition you myself."

Brad felt a strange sensation shoot through his body. More than excitement. More than anticipation. Something even more than hope. Almost from the moment he'd given his heart to God at winter camp, he'd prayed that music, that playing the drums, that being part of a band, would be God's will for his life. And for the first time, he sensed it might be. A door had been opened. Just a crack for now, but still open.

"Here." Trevor held out a business card. On the glossy side was his photograph and a website URL, as well as his agent's contact information. On the plain white back side of the card, Trevor had scribbled his cell phone number and e-mail address. "You keep in touch. Let me know how you're doing."

"You mean it?" Brad looked up from the card, eyes wide.

Trevor grinned. "Yeah, I mean it." Softly — probably not meaning for Brad to hear — he added, "Call me crazy, but I mean it."

CHAPTER 13

The clock on Penny's nightstand said it was 4:00 a.m. Much too early to be awake. But she'd already tossed and turned for a good half hour, trying to force herself back to sleep. It hadn't worked.

With a groan of frustration, she rolled onto her side and turned on the lamp. Then she returned to her back and pulled sheets and blankets up to her chin while staring at the ceiling. Although she attempted to turn her thoughts in other directions, they returned to the previous evening, to the moment when Trevor had led her away from the group and folded her into his arms as she wept. It had seemed a safe place for a time. But then he'd stepped away. Not just physically. It had been more than that. He'd moved away emotionally too. Something that had never happened before, no matter how coldly she'd treated him.

I deserved it.

Funny, wasn't it? She'd done her best to drive him away. Now it seemed she was getting what she'd wanted. And . . . she didn't like it one bit.

Brad wouldn't like it either. Brad would want us to be friends.

Thinking of her brother reminded her of his gift to her last Christmas. She pushed aside the blankets and got out of bed. In the minutes that followed, she searched for the CD. None of the drawers in her bedroom produced it, so she put on her robe and bedroom slippers and made her way downstairs to the entertainment center in the living room, pausing long enough to plug in the tree lights. They sent a lovely, multicolored glow into the room.

It didn't take her much longer to find what she searched for. It was beside the stereo. The cellophane wrapping had been removed from the jewel case, and she wondered how often her dad had listened to the album over the last year. He'd never said a word to her about it. Her heart ached at the discovery. They could have shared this, but she'd been too angry.

With a sigh, she reached for the portable CD player her dad sometimes used — she'd tried to convince him to use his iPad but he'd declined — and went to sit on the

215

couch. She opened the case and popped out the CD, then dropped it into the player. After hooking her hair behind her ears, she put in the earbuds and pressed Play.

The first track was a well-known love song, but Trevor made it distinctly his. The smooth sound of his voice pulled her into the romance of the lyrics. She pictured him sitting on a tall stool, guitar resting on one thigh. For the briefest of moments, she imagined him singing to her. Longing rose up inside of her. Longing to be loved in that same way, for someone special to want to say those same words in the song about her and to her.

She swallowed the lump in her throat, surprised by the unfamiliar feelings swirling inside. But it was a momentary foolishness. She'd never been in a hurry to fall in love. She was content to wait until it was meant to happen. No ticking clock for her. She was too practical for that.

She pushed the Stop button on the player, not waiting for the song to end, and removed the earbuds. Her gaze went to the Christmas tree, staring at the twinkling lights, hoping they would comfort her. Oddly enough, they did just that. For a short while, time stood still. Her thoughts drifted in a sea of silence.

"Penny?" Her father stepped out of the dark hall and into the living room. "What are you doing up so early?"

"I woke up and couldn't go back to sleep." She held up the jewel player. "I was listening to music."

Her dad moved to the couch, picked up the jewel case, and sat beside her. "Trevor's CD, huh?"

"I thought it was about time I listened to it."

"He's good."

"Better than I expected. Even though Brad told me a hundred times at least."

A soft grunt was his only reply.

"Dad?"

"Hmm?"

"Weren't you ever angry with Brad for abandoning us the way he did? For abandoning you and the ranch?"

He placed his arm around her shoulders. "He didn't abandon me, Penny, or you or the ranch. He went after his dream. That's what I raised both of you to do. I raised you to live your own lives, not to live mine."

What her dad said was true. That was how he'd raised his children. But didn't those children have an obligation to him in return?

"I would never want you to stay in Kings Meadow because of me, Pen. If your heart pulled you elsewhere, I would want you to go."

She frowned in frustration. Her dad couldn't manage the ranch without help, and he needed her income as well. Didn't he understand that by now?

"Penny, I would never clip your wings after teaching you how to fly." He tightened his arm, drawing her nearer.

She thought of her brother again — and of Trevor. Both of them so passionate about their music, both of them going after a career in entertainment even when common sense and family members opposed their decisions. Had she ever wanted anything that much? No, she answered herself honestly. She hadn't. Oh, she was content being a librarian. It appealed to her love of order and logic and learning. But was it a passionate dream to be pursued?

"What's troubling you, Pen?"

As she laid her head against his shoulder, she felt that earlier longing rise up inside her again. "I don't know," she whispered. Not a lie. Not really the truth.

He pressed his cheek against the top of her head, and they sat in silence, both lost in their own thoughts.

Trevor had finished his breakfast and was

carrying his dishes to the sink when the phone rang. This early in the morning, the sound sent a shard of anxiety through him as he reached to answer it. "Hello?"

"Trevor. It's Rodney. Glad I caught you before you left."

"I was just about to head your way."

"Well, no need to come unless it's to see your mom. Penny was up early, so she's going to help me with the first feeding."

"Is Mom up?"

"No," Rodney answered. "Not yet."

"You sure you don't need me?"

"I'm sure. But we'll see you tonight."

"All right, then. See you tonight." Trevor heard the click on the opposite end of the wire, then placed the handset back in its cradle.

He washed his breakfast dishes but, once done, was left with lots of time to kill until he had to leave for work. Habit drew him to the black case in the corner. He laid it on the floor, opened it, and removed the guitar. He held it but didn't play it. Not right away. He just let himself draw pleasure from holding the instrument.

But it was different from the kind of pleasure he used to get from it. In the past, playing and singing had been about earning the approval of the audience. He'd needed the applause the way everybody else needed oxygen. He was smart enough to understand at least some of that was due to the difficult relationship he'd had with his father, and it had made him make a host of dumb choices through the years.

Brad used to tell him that God wanted to heal the hurts from his past; that God wanted to be the father who would never betray him or hurt him or reject him. Trevor hadn't believed that was possible. Recent weeks had proven otherwise.

He strummed a few chords as the words of a worship song from church played in his memory. That was an example of another change. He'd spent the last dozen years singing or writing songs about the love between a man and a woman, but the truth was he'd known little about that emotion. Now God was opening his eyes to a greater kind of love, and he found he wanted to sing about it all the time.

His fingers stilled, and for a short while he simply sat in God's presence. From his days in Sunday school, he remembered the words *"Be still, and know that I am God."*

But then, out of nowhere, he thought of Penny. He remembered her tears. He remembered how right it had felt to hold her and comfort her. And he remembered knowing that this wasn't the time to want what he shouldn't want.

Another ring of the telephone was a welcome interruption. He set the guitar aside and answered it. "Hello?"

"Trevor, it's Yuli. I just had a breakfast meeting with the mayor, and I've got some good news for you. We decided that unless we get another major snowstorm, you won't need to come in to work until next Monday. A skeleton crew is all we need the rest of the week. Enjoy the time you've got with your mother and have a merry Christmas."

More time to spend with his mom. More time to spend at the ranch. And, though he tried not to think it, more time to spend with Penny.

"Thanks, Yuli. I appreciate it. Merry Christmas to you too."

After ending the call, his gaze swept the small apartment again. Not a single reason to hang around here, he decided. He grabbed his keys, put on his coat and hat, and headed out the door.

CHAPTER 14

Standing beneath the spray of hot water, Penny shampooed away the bits of hay and dust that had worked their way into her hair, despite her knit cap. Then she stood still and enjoyed the warmth as it seeped into her bones. She never minded helping her dad with the cattle and other chores, but she wasn't a fan of the predawn temperatures of winter.

When she was finished in the shower, she got ready for work with her usual efficiency. Her hair care was low maintenance, as was her makeup routine. In less than half an hour she was headed downstairs.

Laughter from the kitchen greeted her. Her dad and Dot Reynolds. Already the sound seemed familiar to Penny. Then she heard another voice. Trevor's. The song she'd listened to earlier immediately echoed in her mind. Her heart seemed to stop and then race. She'd heard her dad call Trevor on the phone earlier. She'd heard him say Trevor needn't come over this morning. Why was he here? And wasn't he late for work already?

Drawing a steadying breath, she descended the final few steps and walked into the kitchen, as calm and cool as she pleased.

"Ah," her dad said. "Here's Penny now."

She glanced toward the table, acknowledged all three with a smile and a nod of her head, and then poured herself another cup of coffee.

"Ready for some breakfast?" Her dad stood.

She waved him back down. "I'll fix it, Dad. Thanks."

While she heated the skillet, scrambled herself an egg, and buttered a slice of toast, she listened to Dot and Trevor reminisce about some of his boyhood Christmases. Despite the laughter that sometimes accompanied the conversation, Penny sensed Trevor's memories weren't all as merry as he pretended. Something in the tone of his voice. She glanced over her shoulder. Something about his expression too.

With the plate of food in one hand and a small glass of orange juice in the other, she went to the table.

Her dad said, "Trevor doesn't have to go

223

to work again until after Christmas. Where do you think he should take Dot today, Penny? We've got the sleigh ride at the Leonard ranch tonight."

"We can't go far," Trevor interjected. "Have to be here to help you feed."

Her dad frowned. "I don't like interfering with your mother's visit. I appreciate your help, but I can manage on my own when I have to. I've been doing it for a long time."

A protest rose in Penny's throat, but before she could give it voice, Dot spoke.

"Please, you two. I don't need to be entertained." The woman looked first at Penny's dad, then at Trevor. "I am perfectly happy to stay right here and just *be* with you. With *all* of you. I can't tell you how nice it has been to have these leisurely days."

Her dad didn't look convinced yet.

Trevor took hold of his mom's hand at the corner of the table. "Rodney, I can promise you that my mom means whatever she says. We're going to stick close to the ranch."

The tension in Penny's shoulders released a little, and she was glad she'd remained silent. Her dad didn't like it when she fussed over him. He'd made that abundantly clear. Still, if he wanted to avoid back surgery, he needed to heed the surgeon's warnings.

That meant less physical labor. He was doing so much better. He didn't want to mess himself up again.

Let Trevor help.

She almost smiled at how her thinking had changed. First she'd hated him and wanted him gone. Then she'd grudgingly accepted his presence. And now . . . now . . .

As if he knew her thoughts, Trevor looked at her. Their gazes met, and in her mind she once again heard him singing the lyrics from his album. Her stomach tumbled in response. Appetite swept away, she picked up her breakfast dishes and carried them to the sink. After a quick scrape and rinse, she put plate, glass, and table service into the dishwasher. By the time she was done, the unwelcome reaction had abated, and she was able to look toward the table again.

"I'm off," she said, relieved that both her voice and smile were steady. "Have a fun day, whatever you all decide to do."

Her dad said, "We'll eat dinner early, so come straight home from work."

"I will." With a little wave, she left the kitchen, wishing with every step that she hadn't listened to Trevor's CD that morning.

While Trevor mucked a couple of stalls, his

mom and Rodney visited, their voices soft in the dim light of the barn. Trevor grinned to himself as he listened to their easy conversation. They sounded like lifelong friends instead of people who'd been strangers until a few days ago. He guessed that shouldn't surprise him. Rodney had made him feel the same way from day one.

Trevor paused in his work and looked across the barn to where the older couple sat, Rodney on a stool near the workbench and his mom on a folded tarp atop a couple of bales of straw. Winter sunlight filtered through spaces in the slats of wood, highlighting dust motes floating in the air and painting a kind of crown in his mom's brown hair.

When was the last time he'd seen her look as relaxed and happy as she did now? A long time. Many years. As a kid, Trevor had heard his dad belittle his mom almost as often as he did it to him. After he left home for Nashville, Trevor's rare visits home had filled his mom with tension — despite how much she wanted him there — because she'd known a fight between father and son was inevitable. Many fights, even when the visit was brief. In the years since his father's death, she'd had to learn to live alone, to do things she'd never had to do when his dad was alive. That had been more difficult for her than she'd admitted to Trevor, but he'd figured it out on his own.

She was different now. Was it being here in Kings Meadow or was it a change that had happened over time? Perhaps it was a little of both.

Trevor smiled as he resumed cleaning out the second stall. A sense of well-being wrapped around him with the warmth of a down-filled coat. The praise song he'd thought of earlier this morning came to mind again, and he began to whistle it softly.

"Trevor." His mom's voice drew his attention toward the stall door, and he was surprised to find her so close. "That's a song you should record. You should do an entire album of worship music."

What a crazy idea. The album he and the guys had recorded some years back hadn't exactly been a runaway hit, despite everything he'd tried. Consumers of Christian music wouldn't even know who he was. If he couldn't sell country, he couldn't sell anything.

"Think about it," she added with a smile. "I'm going in the house to start supper."

Rodney appeared at her side. "I told her she's our guest and shouldn't do the cooking, but I'm learning she has a stubborn streak."

Trevor couldn't hold back a short laugh of agreement.

"Watch it," his mom said, pointing a finger at him, "or I'll burn something meant for you."

"Hey! *I'm* not the one who called you stubborn."

Her face lit with a smile. "I know." Then she walked away, soft laughter trailing behind her.

After a few moments of silence, Rodney said, "Your mother's a joy."

Trevor couldn't have argued even if he'd wanted to. His mom *was* a joy. She'd been the anchor in a home often consumed by stormy seas, and he felt a surge of love for her. He was glad for the chance to see her looking . . . looking what? The word came to him in an instant: she looked *carefree*. Another reason — one among many — to be thankful to the Cartwrights. And to God.

Trevor leaned the pitchfork against the wall of the barn. "I'm finished here. What else needs done?"

"Nothing, son. Let's go inside and get warm while we wait for Penny's return. Big night ahead."

"I'll bring in Harmony first so Penny

won't have to do it when she gets home from work. I'll join you and Mom in a bit."

"All right."

Trevor reached for his coat that he'd laid over the top rail of the stall. He hadn't needed it while he mucked the stalls, but he knew he would need it when he went out the back door of the barn. Once his coat was buttoned closed, he took the pitchfork in hand again and returned it to where all of the tools were stored before heading outside.

Although technically still afternoon, the promise of evening had dimmed the bright blue of the winter sky. It wouldn't be long before the evening star was visible.

Arriving at the pasture fence, he whistled, although it wasn't necessary. He'd been seen already. Harmony trotted toward him, followed by the two other horses that shared this paddock, all of them counting on a treat of some kind. They weren't disappointed this time. He had carrots in his pocket and distributed them quickly. Then he led Harmony out of the pasture and into the barn.

If he bought a horse while he was in Kings Meadow, what would he do with it once he returned to Nashville? Sure, he could rent a pasture as he had before, but after he began touring, then what? He wouldn't be around enough to enjoy it. Why have the expense if he rarely got to ride?

As he gave Harmony's neck a final pat before heading to the house, it occurred to him that the idea of being back on the road, playing music in smoky venues or at noisy fairs and festivals, held little appeal. The discovery unsettled him. All he'd ever wanted was to make it big in the country music business. The pursuit of fame had been like a drug to him, something he needed as much as food or sleep. Without his quest for stardom, who was he? What was he?

He didn't know, but he knew he'd better find out.

Brad
2011

"Hey, Dad!" Brad hopped up from the desk in his bedroom and carried his laptop with him out into the hallway. "Where are you?"

"In the kitchen."

He hurried down the stairs. "Listen to this. I finally got a reply from Trevor Reynolds." He looked at the screen. " 'Hey, kid. Sorry it took so long for me to answer your last e-mail. I needed to wait until we nailed down a few more dates. Afraid the news is Lincoln, Nebraska, is as far west as we'll make it this summer.' "

He glanced up at his dad, then continued reading. " 'Congrats on graduating from high school with honors, and thanks for the video you sent from that party you played with your friends. You're good. When you get to college, don't let your practice slide. Take care and stay in touch. Trevor.' "

He looked up again. "Did you hear what he said? He liked the video. He thought I played good."

"I heard."

"Man, I wish I could go see him perform again. Maybe you and I could take a trip to Nebraska. You know — a father-son thing. Last hurrah before college." He tried to copy the pleading look his sister could do with ease.

His dad laughed. "Nice try, son."

Sure. He'd known it was a long shot, with or without the pleading look. Money was tight. His dad had used what little there was to spare to see Penny get her master's degree in Denver. Brad was at home to help tend the livestock. That aspect of ranch life had kept his dad on a short leash for years. But the ranch was his dad's passion just like the drums were Brad's. His dad didn't mind the sacrifices he made to live the life he loved. Brad planned to follow his example in pursuit of the life he wanted.

"I was about to make some popcorn," his dad said. "Want some?"

"Sure." Brad closed the laptop and set it on the counter.

"I'll get the air popper. You melt the butter."

"Okay."

His dad opened a cupboard and reached for the popper. "We won't have many more chances to do this before you leave for college."

"Dad, I'm only going to BSU. I'll probably be home so often you'll want to kick me out. And besides, we've got all summer before I leave."

"All summer," his dad echoed softly. "It seems a long time at your age. Not so much at mine."

Brad got butter out of the refrigerator and put some into a coffee mug to melt in the microwave. By the time it was done, the corn was starting to pop into a large mixing bowl on the opposite counter. The sounds and smells brought an onslaught of good memories with them, and Brad suddenly understood that he really would miss home once he was out on his own.

Thanks, God, for making him my dad. He's the best.

CHAPTER 15

The aroma of brewed coffee met Penny the next morning as she entered through the rear door of the library. Not a surprise, since she was a good fifteen minutes late to work. She hadn't been able to get ready this morning with her usual efficiency. After returning from the community sleigh ride at the Leonard ranch the previous evening, the Cartwrights and the Reynoldses had stayed up late, visiting and laughing, Penny included. She'd told herself more than once to go upstairs to bed, but then her dad or Dot or even Trevor had started telling another story and she'd stayed to hear the ending.

"Tired?" Karli asked as she watched Penny hang up her coat. "Here." She held out a cup of coffee. "You look like you need this more than I do."

Penny took it. "Thanks. I do. I didn't take time for any before leaving the house."

"Did you stay at the Leonards' too late?"

"Not really. But it was close to midnight when Trevor finally left the house."

Karli cocked an eyebrow. "You went on the sleigh ride with Trevor Reynolds?"

"Not just with him." She set the coffee mug on the counter. "His mom and my dad too. It was a family affair."

Family? She felt her cheeks grow warm. She'd meant her dad, but it hadn't sounded that way. Then she remembered sitting between her dad and Trevor in the sleigh and the blush intensified. The same blanket had covered her lap and Trevor's. For some reason, it had felt intimate, meaningful, and as inviting as an embrace.

What a silly thing to think.

Trying to sound normal, she said to Karli, "I didn't see you out at the Leonards'. Did you go?"

"No. Stevie started running a fever again." Stevie was Karli's toddler son. "We decided not to expose a babysitter to whatever he has. Although he seemed well enough this morning when I left the house."

"I'm glad to hear he's better. Nobody wants to be sick this time of year. Especially not the little guys."

Karli smiled. "He is in awe of the tree. Doesn't understand about gifts yet. He was too young last Christmas. I'm afraid I went overboard with presents for him this year. It's so hard not to." Her smile faded as she shook her head. "Mitch isn't pleased about the credit-card balance."

Penny didn't have a husband or kids, but she still understood the temptations to overspend at Christmas. Thankfully she'd kept her spending in check this year. To be honest, she'd had little choice.

"Looks like it's time to open the front door." Karli moved away from the counter. "See you out there."

Penny drew in a deep breath, took a sip of her coffee, and then followed Karli out of the break room. She'd just reached the checkout area when the telephone rang. She answered it. "Kings Meadow District Library. Penny speaking."

"Penny. It's Trevor."

Her heart did a strange happy dance in her chest at the sound of his voice. *Ridiculous.*

"Something's wrong with your dad. He collapsed. The paramedics are on the way to the ranch."

Her heart crashed to a halt. "Collapsed? What do you mean? Where was he? What was he doing? Is it his back?"

"It was in the house. He said he wasn't

feeling well, and then he just sort of crum-
pled to the floor."

"He fainted?"

Hesitation, then, "We're not sure. He's
still unconscious."

"No," she whispered.

"We called for the paramedics. They
should be here any minute."

"I'll be right there. I'm coming home
now."

"You might not make it to the ranch in
time."

In time?

"You should meet us at the clinic. I'm sure
they'll want to get him there as fast as they
can and let the doctor decide if he needs to
go to the hospital in Boise."

Clinic. Doctor. Hospital. She felt her
world spinning out of control again.

"Penny?"

Yes, she mouthed, but no sound came
out.

"The paramedics are here."

"I'll meet you at the clinic." She dropped
the handset into the cradle without saying
good-bye. When she turned, she found Karli
standing nearby. "It's my dad."

"I overheard. Go. Go now. I'll take care of
things. Don't give the library a second
thought."

With an abrupt nod, she hurried toward the back exit, fear making it hard to breathe. *Dad. Not Dad. Please not Dad.*

Penny had no idea how long it took her to reach the medical clinic. When she hurried through the double doors, she had no recollection of the route she'd driven or who she might have seen along the way. Nor did she recognize the woman seated at the front desk, although she probably should have.

"I'm Penny Cartwright. Is my dad here? Rodney Cartwright. The ambulance was bringing him in."

The woman — perhaps forty with red hair that had come from a bottle and long, pointy fingernails painted with fluorescent green polish — shook her head. "No, he hasn't arrived. If you'd like to sit over there . . ." She motioned toward some chairs in the waiting area.

Penny would have preferred to pace, but she forced herself to sit down. She even managed to pick up a dog-eared magazine, although she didn't pretend to look at it, let alone thumb through its pages.

She felt a change in air pressure, and instinct told her that the doors at the far end of the corridor had opened. She stood and moved to a place where she could see.

Sure enough, her dad was being rolled into the clinic on a gurney by a couple of paramedics. Behind them came Trevor and his mom. Penny ran down the hallway as they wheeled her dad into a room.

A nurse stopped her before she could follow through the doorway. "You'll have to wait here, Penny."

Penny blinked, once again aware that she should have been able to call the woman by her name. But her mind was blank.

A strong arm went around her shoulders. Softly, Trevor said, "Come on, Penny. Let the doctor tend to your dad. He's in good hands."

She tried to swallow the rising terror but failed.

Gently but persistently, Trevor eased her down the hall until they reached a row of three chairs. He guided her to the middle one. He took the first and his mother settled onto the third. In silence, they shed their coats.

What happened? The question repeated in Penny's head several times, but she hadn't the courage to ask it aloud.

Trevor put his arm around her shoulders once again. She didn't resist. Didn't want to resist. After a while, he drew her closer to his side, and she realized tears were running down her cheeks.

"It's going to be all right," he said softly.

She turned her face into his shirt and allowed fear to form two words in her mind: *Will it?*

Trevor held her, his heart aching. She didn't make a sound as she wept, which made her tears seem all the more tragic. Over Penny's head, his mom watched them, compassion in her eyes. A lump formed in his throat. He was helpless to take away the pain Penny felt, helpless to take away her fears. He knew that but wished he could all the same.

Minutes passed. Long, silent minutes that allowed Trevor's thoughts to roam. He remembered when his father had died, the phone call from his mom, the guilt he'd felt for not caring more. Then he remembered the night he'd held Brad in his arms and watched his life slip away. Brad's loss was one Trevor had mourned deeply — and he'd experienced a different kind of guilt. Now, if Rodney were to die . . .

God, I'm afraid too. Help him, Lord.

Penny drew back from him, sat straight, and dried her eyes with a tissue Trevor's mom pressed into her hand. "Thank you," she whispered.

He withdrew his arm from around her

shoulders, sensing she didn't wish to be comforted by him any longer. He could almost see her put on the armor she would need to win whatever emotional battle awaited her.

Time crawled while they waited in silence, but finally the sounds of footsteps drew their eyes to a doctor in a white coat walking toward them. His gaze swept over the threesome, then settled on Penny. "Miss Cartwright."

She nodded. "Dr. Frederick." Trevor saw her grasp his mom's hand.

"We don't have the results of the blood work yet, but from what your father told me, he was diagnosed with diabetes sometime in the fall. Did he tell you that?"

Penny shook her head, then nodded, then shrugged. "He said his doctor in Boise advised him to watch his blood sugar, but Dad never used the word *diabetic*. I thought cutting back on sugar was a precaution. That he just needed to curb his sweet tooth and watch his weight. That's how he made it sound." She inhaled as she got to her feet. "How serious is it?"

"He wasn't in a diabetic coma, which was our first concern. He's alert and answering all of our questions. We're getting him rehydrated with an IV now, and when we confirm the diagnosis, we'll administer appropriate medications to get his sugars under control."

"Will he need to be transferred to the hospital?"

The doctor shook his head. "I can't say with absolute certainty until the blood work is back and I'm able to speak to his personal physician, but I believe we'll be able to care for him here at the clinic."

"May I see him?"

"Not yet. Give us a while. I'll send the nurse for you when he's ready to have visitors."

Penny sank onto the chair again.

After a brief silence, Trevor asked the doctor, "How long will he need to stay?"

"Two or three days, I imagine. He obviously needs to learn to manage his blood-sugar levels, and Miss Cartwright should be educated too. He must eat the right foods and get the right exercise and take his medications as prescribed. I can recommend a good nutritionist to work with him. But we'll have time to go over all of that later. If you'll excuse me, I'll get back to my patient."

They watched the doctor retrace his steps to the room Rodney was in. Only after Dr. Frederick was out of sight did Penny speak.

"Why didn't Dad tell me the truth?" She turned from Trevor to his mom. "Why did he hide his condition from me?"

"I haven't known your father long," his mom answered with great tenderness, "but I suspect he didn't tell you because he didn't want you to worry about him."

"More than I do already?" Penny clutched her hands in her lap.

His mom gave her the briefest of smiles. "More than you do already."

Penny wanted to be angry with her dad for keeping his condition a secret, but she couldn't muster the emotion. Right now, all she wanted was for him to get well.

What would have happened to him if he'd been alone when he collapsed?

A diabetic coma had been a possibility, according to the doctor. She didn't know much about the disease. Not really. But she did know that a coma wasn't a good thing.

"Penny?" Dot said softly, touching Penny's arm. "Trevor's going back to the ranch to see to the animals. Would you like me to stay here with you or would you prefer to be alone?"

"Please stay," she whispered as she took hold of Dot's hand again.

Trevor stood and reached for his coat. "I'll

be back when everything's done."

Penny nodded. "Trevor . . . I'm so thankful you and your mom were with Dad."

"Me too."

She watched as he headed for the front entrance of the clinic, but once he was out of sight, she discovered she wished him back. She missed the strength she'd felt emanating from him as he sat beside her.

Funny, wasn't it? She'd been so angry with him when he showed up in Kings Meadow. She'd resented the way her dad had accepted him into their home, into their lives. She'd wanted him gone. Even as she'd begun to like him, she'd wanted him to leave Idaho, to go back to Nashville, to go back to the life he had elsewhere. Sooner rather than later.

But because he was in Kings Meadow, because Trevor had been at their ranch, her dad had received the swift attention he'd needed. Perhaps Trevor had saved her dad's life. Had God brought Trevor into their lives for that very purpose?

But if so, if You saved Dad, why couldn't You save Brad too?

Trevor was loading bales of hay onto the back of the flatbed truck when he heard somebody call his name. He rounded the

244

barn and saw Chet Leonard and Grant Nichols standing beside Chet's black truck.

"We came to help," Chet said as Trevor approached them. "How's Rodney?"

"Okay, I think. Or he will be. How did you know he was sick?"

"One of the paramedics told his wife that they took Rodney to the clinic after he blacked out. News spread fast from there. No details, of course, but nobody around here needs details before they pitch in."

"I can see that."

"So what can we do?"

Trevor motioned with his head. "I was about to feed the cattle."

"Let's go, then."

With two strong men on the back of the truck while another took the wheel, they accomplished the task in record time. Afterward, they went into the house. While Trevor made sure the dogs and cat had food and water, Chet and Grant turned off the coffeemaker and the lights that had been left on throughout the house. An intermittent beep from the answering machine drew Trevor toward the telephone. A number in a small display told him there were six messages on the recorder.

Chet said, "Penny's going to have lots of those to listen to when she gets home. And tell her not to worry about food. The women are already getting a schedule together for casseroles and such."

"She'll appreciate it," Trevor said, although he suspected she wouldn't think about food much.

"What time do you need us back this afternoon?" Grant asked.

It was two days before Christmas, and still people found time to help a friend and neighbor in need. Trevor didn't even know his neighbors' names in Nashville. He probably wouldn't recognize them if he met them on the street. He'd always thought he liked it that way. Now he had cause to wonder.

He pushed away the thoughts and answered Grant's question. Then all three went outside and got into their respective trucks, Trevor eager to get back to the clinic . . . and to Penny.

CHAPTER 16

Penny's dad was asleep when she arrived at the clinic the next morning. She took a seat in the chair in the corner and opened her laptop. After connecting it to the clinic's public Wi-Fi, she entered *diabetes* in the search box and began clicking on the links that came up. She'd already brought home most of the books on the library shelves about Type 2 diabetes and had stayed up late the previous night — reading, making notes, and writing down additional titles to borrow or buy.

"It's Christmas Eve," her dad said, his voice scratchy.

She put down the laptop and went to his bedside. "I know."

"This isn't where you should spend it." He gave her a fleeting smile.

She returned it before leaning down to kiss his forehead.

"Did you talk to the doctor when you got

here?" he asked.

She shook her head.

"He says I can go home later this afternoon."

Anxiety tightened her chest. "So soon? Is
he sure that's a good idea?"

"He's sure."

"But, Dad, you —"

"Don't, Penny. We're going to figure all of
this out, but we can do that at home. I don't
need to be lying in this bed, racking up
more medical bills." He took hold of her
hand and squeezed. "I was foolish. I didn't
take my condition seriously. I didn't watch
my diet or take the medication I was supposed to take. That has changed as of right
now. I'll do everything the doctor tells me
to do. I promise you."

Tears welled in her eyes. "You scared me,
Dad."

"I know. I'm sorry for that. Truly I am."

"What if you'd been home alone? What if
you hadn't been found for hours and
hours?"

"But that wasn't what happened, was it?"

They had exchanged similar words yesterday when she'd finally been able to see him.
She took no more comfort from them now
than she had then.

"Sweetheart, why don't you go attend to

whatever you need and come back this afternoon when they release me? You must have a lot to do to be ready for Christmas dinner. We have guests coming."

She felt her eyes widen in surprise. Didn't he have a clue how sick he was? "Dad, we don't have guests coming. Not now. We weren't even sure you'd be home for Christmas. The Leonards invited the Simpsons to their house, so they're taken care of. And Dot took charge of the dinner for the four of us, although if we'd wanted them to, your friends would have brought over everything already prepared."

As her dad's disappointment took hold, he seemed to sink deeper into his pillow.

Penny squeezed his hand. "Nothing matters except that you're on the mend and you'll be home."

"I'm afraid I've ruined Christmas for everyone."

"But you haven't, Dad. You'll see."

He frowned. "I don't suppose peppermint hot chocolate will be on my Christmas menu."

"No way." She nearly launched into a lecture on the evils of processed sugars in the diets of Americans. Then she saw the corners of his mouth twitch as he fought a smile. "Oh, you." She pretended to slap his

249

wrist, even as her own smile blossomed. "Don't you tease me, Dad. Not today."

"I'll be good. I promise. I won't tease you and I won't ask for hot chocolate."

She gave him a serious glance. "Heather has a couple of diabetic cookbooks in the bookstore, and Trevor said he would swing over there to get them today."

Her dad nodded but didn't say anything. Penny wondered if he was thinking of the favorite foods of his that were on the do-not-eat list. She'd certainly thought about their diets — separately and together — and had felt somewhat overwhelmed by the changes ahead.

A rapping sound drew her attention toward the door. As if summoned by the mention of his name, Trevor stood there, holding his hat in one hand. "Am I intruding?"

"Not at all," her dad answered. "Come in."

Trevor stepped to the side of the bed opposite Penny. "How're you feeling, sir?"

"Better. Much better."

Penny moved back to the chair and sat on it, watching the two men together. Her dad's demeanor had perked up even more. There was a small part of her that wanted to resent how close they'd become in so short a time, but even if she'd tried, she wouldn't have been able to muster that old feeling. It was gone. Gone for good.

It wasn't his fault. Not Brad's leaving. Not Brad's dying.

It felt good to admit it, and she supposed it would feel even better once she admitted her error to Trevor. She owed him that much.

From the doorway came another voice. "Knock-knock." Tess Carter stepped into full view. "Hi, Mr. Cartwright. Are you allowed another visitor?"

"Sure." Penny's dad grinned. "Of course. Come in, Tess."

Tess moved to stand beside Trevor, but her gaze went to Penny. She nodded a hello.

Penny returned the nod, trying to ignore the sudden discomfort in her stomach.

"Mr. Cartwright," Tess said, "I was so upset when I heard what happened that I had to come over to make certain you are on the mend." She briefly touched the back of his hand where it lay atop the white blanket.

"I am. In fact, I'm going home later today."

"Oh, that's such good news." Tess turned a smile in Trevor's direction. Then, unexpectedly, she stepped away from him and settled onto a chair next to Penny. "And are

251

you okay, Pen?"

Penny nodded.

"Thank God Trevor was there for you." Tess glanced toward him again, then in a softer voice added, "He cares so much for both you and your dad."

Her friend's words caught Penny by surprise. She'd thought Tess was in pursuit of Trevor, and she'd thought Trevor —

"Good morning, Mr. Cartwright." The nurse — a nononsense sort of woman — stepped into the room on the quiet soles of her clean white shoes.

Seeing the blood glucose meter in the woman's hand, Trevor said, "I'll get out of the way, Rodney. See you this afternoon." To Penny, he said, "Call if you need me for any reason."

"I will."

"He cares so much for both you and your dad."

Although she refused to analyze the reasons why, Penny felt a lightness in her heart that she hadn't felt in days.

Rodney ignored the nurse as she pricked his finger and let the test strip soak up blood. Instead his gaze and his thoughts were on his daughter. He'd suspected it before this, but now he was certain: Penny had come to care for Trevor. More than she understood, perhaps.

If Penny and Trevor fell in love, if they were to marry, he wouldn't have to worry about the future for his daughter. What would happen to Penny if he died? The ranch would go to her, of course, but she hadn't the physical or financial resources to maintain it for long by herself. She would have to sell the livestock, probably sell the ranch itself. And with it gone, would she even want to stay in Kings Meadow? Not likely.

I should have been better prepared. I should have provided more for her future.

Penny wasn't a child, of course. She was a bright and capable young woman. She would find her way no matter what happened to him. Then again, he didn't have to die in order for the ranch to fall into troubled times. A man could only take the help of friends and neighbors for so long before he had to make tough choices.

He could sell the ranch — lock, stock, and barrel — but just the thought of leaving the home where he'd been so happily married, where he and Charlotte had raised their children, almost broke his heart. Memories overwhelmed him.

Penny looked up. Their gazes met. After a

253

moment, she rose from the chair and came to the side of the bed again. Only after she took hold of his hand did he realize the nurse had finished the test and left the room without him noticing.

"What's wrong, Dad? Are you feeling all right?"

"I'm okay, Pen. Just feeling a bit sentimental, that's all."

"Sentimental?"

"It's almost Christmas." True enough, though not the answer to her question.

She squeezed his hand. "You'll be home soon."

After leaving the clinic, Trevor raced through a list of errands — last-minute purchases at the Merc that his mom had requested, getting the wrapped Christmas gifts he'd kept at his apartment along with a change of clothes for later in the day, a stop at the electronics/hardware/video store in the center of town to pick up a couple of DVDs from Mrs. Hansen — before heading back to the ranch. When he opened the door to the mudroom, the air was rich with the scent of baking. His mom, he could tell, was having a busy day.

"Is that you, Trevor?" she called.

"It's me." He stepped into the kitchen and

set the bags of groceries on the nearest counter. "Something smells good."

Cookies were cooling on lengths of aluminum foil. Dozens of cookies. Even more of them — frosted now — were on plates covered in clear plastic wrap, topped with a bright Christmas bow.

"I hope those aren't all for us," he said as he reached for one.

His mom playfully slapped the air near his hand. "You haven't had lunch yet. And, no, they aren't all for us. I don't want too many kinds of the wrong food to tempt Rodney when he gets home. But I thought it would be a nice way of saying thanks to the men who've helped you and will help you with the horses and cattle while Rodney's recuperating." She tilted her head slightly to one side as she looked at him, her eyes narrowing. "But you love the ranch work, don't you?"

"Yeah, I do. Took to it like a duck to water, Rodney says." He was quicker in his reach this time, coming back with an unfrosted snowman in his hand. He grinned in triumph.

His mom tried to look irritated — but failed.

Trevor took a bite of the cookie. "I'm going to get the rest of the stuff out of my truck, then see to some things in the barn. I'll have lunch after the cows are fed."

"Do you know what time they're expected to release Rodney?"

"No." He shook his head. "Just sometime this afternoon."

He returned to his pickup and retrieved the rest of the items from the rear seat — gifts and DVDs in plastic grocery bags, his change of clothes in a duffel bag. Inside the house, he put the gifts under the tree and set the movies on the console holding the DVD player. The duffel bag he left in the entry hall.

A short while later, he entered the barn. Harmony nickered to him from the stall, and he went over to her. "Hey, girl." He stroked the mare's neck — and thought of Penny. But thinking of her had nothing to do with the horse. He'd thought about her a lot lately, throughout the day, every day, no matter what he was doing. He couldn't help himself.

"I'm falling in love with her," he said to Harmony.

The mare bobbed her head, as if in agreement.

"Not exactly the reason God brought me to Kings Meadow." He pressed his forehead to Harmony's, the way he'd seen Penny do.

Of course, he'd arrived in Idaho not truly knowing what he was doing here, beyond keeping a promise he hadn't meant to keep. He'd come to believe he was supposed to be some sort of help to Brad's father and sister, but even that had seemed nebulous in the beginning. Now the purpose of his sojourn in Kings Meadow seemed so much bigger. Here was where he'd truly begun to walk with Christ. Here he'd found friendship and acceptance and forgiveness.

One thing he knew for certain, he hadn't come here to find love.

A line from one of his mom's favorite movies came to him: *A bird may love a fish, but where would they build a home together?"* Loving Penny Cartwright felt as impossible as that bird and that fish.

Or did it? He frowned. "Could it be part of Your will, Lord? Is that another reason I'm here? I need to understand."

With a shake of his head, he backed away from the stall and the horse in it, pivoted on his heel, and headed out of the barn.

It was a quiet Christmas Eve. Just the four of them, Penny and her dad and their two guests. Two guests who had begun to feel more like friends. No, more than that. Like family.

They broke with tradition by staying home from the Christmas Eve communion service and not waiting to open gifts until the next morning. And the surprise for Penny was that she didn't mind breaking tradition. She didn't mind doing something out of the ordinary. Something totally unplanned.

They took turns opening the presents under the tree, beginning with her dad. He loved the fat history book from Trevor, the bag of sugar-free candy and a new tool belt from Dot, and a pair of much-needed work boots from Penny.

Dot exclaimed over the gift from Penny and her dad — a picture of the valley taken many years ago by a renowned photographer who'd lived outside of Kings Meadow. Her delight over Trevor's present was just as obvious. It was a church for her miniature village collection, apparently one she had been wanting for a long time.

Trevor got a pair of leather gloves from his mom, along with a gift card to a music store, and a belt with a fancy silver buckle from the Cartwrights. The buckle had been her dad's idea, and Penny hadn't been any too happy at the time. It had seemed too extravagant . . . especially for him. But she didn't feel that way anymore.

As for Penny, the gift from her dad made

her laugh — a feminine version of the pair of boots she'd given him and exactly what she'd wanted. From Dot, she received a scarf that would dress up any outfit, the colors perfect for her wardrobe.

She opened Trevor's present last. She hadn't any expectations for what he might give her and yet felt a strange anticipation as she removed the ribbon, bow, and wrapping paper. Inside was a large shoe box, but she doubted he'd bought her the men's athletic shoes displayed on the side of the box. Curiosity growing, she lifted the lid. Inside were two sky-blue beaded halters, one for an adult horse, the other fit for a foal.

Trevor leaned toward her. "Hope it doesn't feel like I gave Harmony the gift instead of you."

Her heart thrummed a crazy beat as she lifted her gaze to meet his. "Of course not. I love them."

"I got them because they're the same color as your eyes," he added softly, so only she could hear.

Strange. It almost felt as if those words were his real gift to her.

BRAD

2012

"It's none of your business, Penny. Stay out of it." Brad slammed out of the house, his anger continuing to boil as he walked to the truck, hopped in, and drove away.

It had been like this all summer between him and his sister. Their dad had spent a lot of time playing referee between the two, to no avail. It wasn't as if Brad hadn't tried to keep his temper, tried to mend fences, tried to get back to the way things used to be between him and Penny. But nothing he'd tried ever worked for long.

Their latest fight had started when she'd repeated — for what seemed the millionth time — her plans for his life after he graduated from Boise State. That was still three years away, but she acted like the future was etched in stone — and *she* was the stone-cutter.

He'd made the mistake of saying, "I don't know what I'll do or where I'll go after college. I may want to take a job someplace besides here or Boise. I'm thinking about Nashville." He should have known better than to mention Nashville. It was code for "country music," and they both knew it.

Things had escalated quickly from there, Penny calling him selfish, Brad calling her a control freak. He'd left before either of them could say anything worse.

Arriving at a parking area that led to the river, Brad found a place in the shade and cut the engine. Then he got out of the truck and started walking. Fast. With any luck he could burn off the anger and frustration with a good hike.

Maybe he'd been wrong to listen to Penny's urging to go for an engineering degree. Maybe that had given her the idea that she was in charge — that he would do whatever she told him to do. It wasn't too late to change his major. He could study music.

"You'd end up a teacher, Brad," Penny's voice echoed in his memory. *"You've never said you want to teach. Do you?"*

No, it wasn't what he wanted. But neither did he want to be an engineer just so he could get a job that paid lots of money. He wanted to be a drummer. He wanted to live and work with other musicians. Why couldn't she understand that?

He halted on the path along the riverbank. Closing his eyes, he drew in a long, deep breath and let it out slowly. Once, twice, then a third time.

I shouldn't let her get to me that way. I should hold my temper. She's just trying to help.

He opened his eyes and looked at the sky. "Okay. So how do I make things better?"

Leave for college now!

That wasn't an answer from God. That was his own thought. And not the right answer. Not really. If he —

Meooow.

He looked around.

Meooow.

He hadn't imagined the sound. It was a kitten. A kitten in distress. He stepped off the beaten path and began poking through the underbrush.

Meooow.

He found the black-and-white kitten at the base of a pine tree, clinging to the trunk only a few inches above the ground. He doubted it was more than six or eight weeks old.

"Hey, look at you. How'd you get all the way out here all by yourself?"

The most probable answer was that the

262

kitten had been dumped here. Or maybe it had escaped being drowned in the river. He knew people did that kind of thing, although he couldn't understand how they could. Slowly he reached out and gently pulled the kitten off the tree trunk. It wasn't any too happy, but it was too small to escape his grasp. He turned it around to face him.

"Hey, look at that tuxedo you're wearing. Aren't you a handsome guy? Oops, I think maybe you're a girl. That's okay. I like girls." He grinned. "We'll call you Tux. What do you think of that?"

Meooow.

Brad laughed as he drew the kitten close to his chest. "Yeah. Things are tough all over. But you won't feel that way when we get home and I get you full of milk."

Imagining Penny's expression when she saw he'd brought home a kitten made him laugh again. His sister tried to like cats but never quite succeeded. Still, maybe Tux would make her forget their latest fight. He could only hope.

CHAPTER 17

The following six days passed in a blur. Trevor was at the ranch more than he was not and felt more and more at home there. With Rodney's neighbors pitching in, the chores never seemed to take long, which left more time for him to spend with his mom — and when she wasn't at the library, with Penny. Rodney began to feel stronger with each passing day, faster than anyone had expected, including Rodney himself. He adjusted to the lifestyle changes required of him without complaint. Finally the day arrived for Trevor to drive his mom to the Boise airport for her flight home. Rodney joined him for the drive there and back. He said it was to keep Trevor company. Trevor thought the older man just wanted a couple more hours with Dot. The two had become fast friends.

Trevor had just returned to his apartment after dropping Rodney at the ranch when his telephone rang.

"Hey, Trev. How the heck are you?"

It took him a few seconds to recognize the voice. Not because it wasn't a familiar one, since it belonged to one of his original band members, Beck Thompson, but it had been a while since they'd talked. Beck had left the band when his wife got pregnant with the first of their three kids. The youngest of them must be three or four years old by now.

"I'm good, Beck. Doing all right. How about you?"

"Good. Great. Wife's fine. Kids are fine. Listen, I've been calling your cell phone and sending texts for a couple of weeks. Don't you ever answer? I finally got this number from your agent."

"My mobile phone doesn't work up here in these mountains. Guess I should call in for my messages via my landline."

"Yeah. You should. This is important."

Trevor shucked out of his coat and settled onto a chair. "What's up?"

"Well, it's kind of a long story, but the short version is I met a producer who I think might be able to do something for you."

How often had Trevor heard words like those before? Seemed like dozens of times in a dozen years. He would hear them, get

265

his hopes up, and then nothing would happen. Nothing big anyway. Nothing that had catapulted him to where he'd wanted to be.

"Trevor, you ought to think about coming back to Nashville."

Penny's image flashed in his head. He saw her tender smile. Heard her sweet laugh.

"Are you listening, Trev? 'Cause I'm serious as a heart attack. Get back here. Don't walk away from everything."

"I'm not walking away," he answered emphatically — and then wondered if it was true. He drew in a slow breath. "I came to Idaho to keep a promise to Brad. I'm helping out his dad and sister."

"So how long's that gonna take?"

"I don't know for sure. A while."

The silence from Beck's end of the call almost crackled with displeasure.

Trevor tried to give a better answer. "A month or two." But that didn't sound long enough. "Maybe by the end of March."

"Okay, listen. I'm gonna keep working on things at this end. But you need to tell me how I can reach you without a long lag time, in case something breaks all of a sudden."

Even my agent isn't this persistent. Trevor almost laughed. "Tell you what: if you can't reach me here at this number, call and leave a message on my cell. I promise to check for messages every night before I turn in. Good enough?"

"Guess it'll have to be. You start thinking about getting back here before March. I'll call you when I know anything more."

And I won't be holding my breath until then. "Sure. Sounds good. Take care, Beck."

"You too, Trevor."

By the next day, Trevor had almost forgotten Beck's phone call. In the past he would have dwelt on the possibilities every waking hour and probably dreamed about them too. It just wasn't the end-all and be-all anymore, as amazing as that was for him to admit. He pondered that bit of self-discovery as he kicked snow off his boots after feeding the cattle. Once in the mud-room, he removed his coat and hung it on a peg on the wall, then walked into the kitchen.

Seated at the table, Rodney looked up. "You done already?" Spread before him was a ledger book, a pile of receipts and invoices, and a calculator.

"Yes, sir." Trevor crossed the room and sat on a chair opposite the older man.

"Wish you'd let me help. I'm perfectly capable of driving that truck again."

"Help was already lined up through next

weekend. Let's leave things as they are. It won't hurt you to keep resting until then."

"You're almost as bossy as my daughter," Rodney grumbled, but a chuckle spoiled the effect.

Trevor pointed at the paperwork on the table. "Looks like you've got enough on your hands for now, anyway."

The older man sighed, his gaze locked on a page of the ledger. "At the moment, I'm robbing Peter to pay Paul."

"Doesn't sound good."

"It's not."

Trevor leaned forward on his chair. "Is there anything I can do to help?"

"No, son. You've already done so much."

He hesitated to ask the obvious question. He didn't want to insult Rodney or intrude where he shouldn't. He respected the man, trusted him, wouldn't want to offend him in any way. But the question rolled around in his head until it would no longer be ignored. "Sir, do you need to borrow money?"

Rodney looked up and seemed about to deny it. Then, with a slow shake of his head, he said, "The bank already turned me down for a loan. And that was before my stay at the clinic. I suppose I'm an even poorer risk now."

"I didn't mean from the bank. I could loan you some money."

Silence gripped the kitchen for a long time before Rodney answered, "No, Trevor. I couldn't accept it. But thank you. I appreciate the offer. More than I can say."

Trevor wasn't going to be so easily refused. Not now that he'd warmed to the idea. "Think about it, Rodney. I'm not rich, but I've got a fair-sized nest egg in the bank. My expenses are almost nothing here in Kings Meadow. Even less than I thought they'd be when I first arrived. It wouldn't be a burden on me. You don't have to worry about that. I promise. I wouldn't offer if I didn't have it to give. Maybe I don't have enough to cover everything you need, but surely it would be enough to help see you through until you can sell off more calves." He saw Rodney was about to reply, suspected he was about to refuse again. "Don't answer right this instant. Don't refuse until you think about it. Really think about it."

Silent as requested, Rodney ran the fingers of his right hand through his gray hair.

Trevor leaned back, afraid that if he left the room, Rodney would talk himself out of accepting the offer. And Trevor really wanted him to accept. Wanted it more with each passing minute.

The sound of the door opening and closing broke the quiet that had settled over the
two men. A moment later Penny's voice
called out, "I forgot to tell you the library
was closing early, Dad."

Trevor glanced toward the door as she
walked into the kitchen. Her cheeks were
rosy, as if she'd been a long while in the
cold instead of only the moments it took to
go from car to house. Her smile seemed
directed at Trevor as well as her dad, and it
felt good that it didn't vanish the way it used
to when she looked at him.

"I thought I'd go for a ride," she said. "I
haven't been in the saddle in ages, and
everything is so beautiful with the sunshine
sparkling off the snow and the sky such an
icy blue."

"It's mighty cold out there," Rodney said.

"I'll bundle up good." Her gaze met
Trevor's. "Would you like to join me?"

"You bet." He stood so fast his chair
started to tip over. He grabbed for it just in
time.

Amusement twinkled in her eyes. "I'll run
up to change my clothes." She disappeared
through the doorway.

Trevor sat down again.

"She always did like riding horses in the
cold and snow." Rodney gave Trevor a

270

knowing look. "Seems you agree with her. As for me, I think I'll go sit by the fire and take a nap."

Penny's and Trevor's breaths hung before their faces as they saddled and bridled their mounts. But Penny barely noticed the cold. She was dressed for the weather, of course, but the reason she didn't notice went beyond that. She felt . . . happy. A happiness that warmed her much more than the insulated underwear beneath her jeans and sweater. She had no interest in analyzing why she felt happy, only in enjoying it.

The horses ready, they led them out of the barn. Trevor closed the door behind them before stepping into the saddle. "Where are we headed?" he asked as his gaze swung in her direction.

She pointed toward the eastern mountains with an outstretched arm. "Thataway." Then she nudged her horse's sides with her heels and they started forward. "Come on, Fred. Ginger."

The two border collies didn't need further encouragement.

Trevor had mentioned that he wanted to own a horse again, and she realized, when she looked over at him, that she'd been skeptical about his interest. She shouldn't have been. The way he sat in the saddle, the way he held the reins, the pleasure written in the upward turn of the corners of his mouth — all said he hadn't embellished his experience with horses or the enjoyment he took from them.

We should have done this before today.

Trevor glanced her way. She wished the sunglasses didn't hide his eyes.

"This is great," he said, grinning. "Thanks for inviting me to come along. I'll be sore tomorrow, but I'm loving it now."

You look good in the saddle. Her cheeks grew warm.

Perhaps not noticing her blush, he looked across the fields toward the mountains again. "I haven't been out this direction before. It's the visual definition of *winter wonderland,* isn't it?"

"I think so."

"How far along this way is Cartwright land?"

She pointed ahead. "That clump of trees is the northeast corner. Beyond that fence line, there's about sixty acres that have been for sale for the last five years. Dad's always wished he could buy that land so he could increase the herd. But the owners haven't lowered the price any in five years, so I guess they aren't in a hurry to sell." She shrugged. "It doesn't matter now. Can't afford it. And growing the ranch is the last thing Dad needs to do for his health."

"He wants it because he's the real deal. You know what I mean. A modern-day cowboy. It isn't about the clothes he wears. It's the land and the livestock. It runs in his veins, I think."

"Dad would love to hear you say all that."

"Well, it's true. Me, all I've got are the boots, jeans, and hat. Oh, and the pickup truck."

She smiled at him. "You forgot your love of country music. That's worth a point or two of cowboy cred."

"Cowboy *cred*?" He laughed aloud. "Did a librarian really say that? Isn't it sort of a mixed metaphor or something? You know. The word *cowboy* mixed with urban lingo."

She feigned insult. "I like it." But she couldn't keep it up for long. Her laughter bubbled up to mingle with his.

They fell into a pleasant silence; the only sounds the crunch of crusty snow beneath the horses' hooves and the creak of leather saddles. Sunlight sparkled across the snowy landscape. At the foot of the mountains, smoke rose from a chimney, although the house itself was hidden from view. Penny thought she caught a whiff of burning wood,

273

although it was probably her imagination. That chimney was a long way off, and the air was still, no breeze to carry scents any distance.

"Tell me something," Trevor said.

She glanced over at him. "What?"

"If it weren't for your father, would you still be living in Kings Meadow?"

She pondered the question for a short while, finally answering, "I don't know. If you'd asked me a few years ago, I would have said no. Not because I don't like it here. I *love* it. But I wanted to see more of the country while I was young and unmarried."

"Did you ever come close to marrying? Any special guy in your life?"

It surprised her, the personal nature of his questions, and yet she wasn't upset or even reluctant to answer. "No. Not really. There was somebody I dated in college for a number of months. I thought the relationship might turn into something special. But it never did. On either of our parts. We were better as friends. You know what I mean."

A shrug was his answer.

"Have *you* ever thought about marrying?"

He answered quickly and firmly. "No. Never." Once again his gaze lifted to the mountaintops ahead of them. "My parents' marriage wasn't the happiest I've seen. My dad was a . . . He was a hard man. Angry. Unkind." He drew a breath. "He could be cruel at times."

She'd guessed as much as she'd grown to know Trevor, but it hurt to hear him say the words aloud. "And because of that, you don't ever want to marry?"

"You know how they say cycles get repeated, passed along in families. Like adult children of alcoholics becoming alcoholics. Like those kids who were abused become abusers. What if I got married and had kids and ended up treating my wife and children the way Mom and I were treated?"

"It doesn't have to be that way, Trevor. Dad always says that God can break generational sins."

He looked at her, emotions flickering across his face. It seemed as if he wanted to believe her but was afraid to. After a long while, he said, "The life of a traveling musician isn't exactly conducive to healthy, long-term relationships. Of any kind. Romantic or otherwise. It always seemed best that I just keep my friendships casual."

"Sounds lonely."

He glanced her way again. "I never used to think so."

"And now?"

Again he shrugged. "Guess I'm not so sure."

Why did that answer make her pulse quicken?

As if needing her body to move as fast as her heart rate, she tapped the heels of her boots against her gelding's sides. The horse broke into a trot, the dogs running ahead. Trevor lagged behind only for a short while. When his mount pulled up beside her, he grinned but seemed content for them to lapse into silence once again.

It suited Penny as well.

CHAPTER 18

Hours later, the sky had grown overcast, and the mercury had dipped sharply. Trevor and Penny led their mounts into the barn to unsaddle them. Rodney joined them before the cinches were completely undone.

"Have a good time?" the older man asked, leaning against the rails of a stall.

"Yes," they answered in unison.

That caused Trevor to smile. He liked the sound of their voices blended together.

"Where did you go?"

Penny answered, "We rode as far as the old Riverton estate."

Rodney's eyebrows arched. "That far? No wonder you were gone so long."

"It didn't seem all that long." Trevor lifted the saddle from his mount's back. "And it was great to see the valley from horseback. Whole different perspective than I get driving around in my truck."

Rodney nodded as he pushed off the stall.

"You know, you two ought to think about doing something fun for New Year's Eve. You've been trapped inside taking care of me for much too long. That is, when you aren't outside tending the livestock."

"Dad, I don't think —"

"You could go down to Boise to see a movie. At the very least, you should go have yourself a nice dinner at the Tamarack Grill. In fact, I called and made a reservation for you two at eight o'clock, just in case you'd want to do that. I heard Grant Nichols has a special menu for tonight, and supposedly they've got a treat in mind for those who stick around until midnight to see in the New Year."

"But, Dad, if we go out to eat, you should come with us."

He shook his head. "No, I think I'd better stick close to my own kitchen for a while. You know, watch the diet and all. But you young folk should go and enjoy yourselves."

Rodney Cartwright was about as subtle as a freight train, Trevor thought, but since the older man was suggesting the exact thing Trevor had wanted to ask Penny himself, he didn't object. Maybe he could even help things along.

"Let's do it, Penny," he said, looking at her over the back of the horse between

278

them. "It'll be fun."

Indecision played across her face.

"Come on," he pressed. "Let's make it a date. We can dress up and do the town." He tried to sound playful, teasing, as if the invitation was all in fun. After all, *doing the town* in Kings Meadow would not make for much excitement, even on this night of the year. But he was dead serious about it being a date. Would she realize that? And if she did, would it scare her off or be what she wanted?

The waiting was close to agony.

"All right." Her voice was soft and perhaps a little uncertain, but despite that, she'd agreed to go out with him.

"Great!" He looked at Rodney again. "I'll get the cattle fed and then go home to shower and change."

Two and a half hours later, Trevor drove toward the Cartwright ranch again. Except for a little white trim on his shirt, he was dressed all in black, from the cowboy hat on his head to the boots on his feet. It had been one of his favorite outfits to wear when he performed. He hoped Penny would like it too. He wanted to impress her. He wanted her to find him attractive. With Penny, everything seemed to matter.

279

He silently prayed for God's will to be done, then felt a twinge of fear. What if God's will wasn't for Penny to fall in love with him? He knew he was supposed to want God's will above everything else, but praying for it when he wasn't assured of the outcome was more difficult than he'd expected it would be.

"I already love her, Lord," he whispered. "Sure would be great if she could love me too."

Arriving at the ranch, he drove to his usual parking spot and cut the engine. As he exited the truck and climbed the porch steps, he felt as nervous as a teenager on his first date. He didn't enter the house of his own accord as had become his habit over the past couple of weeks. Instead he knocked and waited.

Rodney answered it. "Don't you clean up good."

"I did my best, sir."

The older man pulled the door open wide. "Come on in. Penny isn't down yet."

"Thanks." Trevor stepped into the entry hall, but before he could remove his hat or coat, a sound drew his gaze to the top of the stairs.

Penny stood there, wearing a dress that seemed both simple and formal. Sky blue, like her eyes and the gift he'd given her for Christmas. Silver threads in the fabric sparkled in the lamplight. Her long blonde hair had been swept up on her head and was adorned with a slender sequined band. It wasn't a tiara, but it seemed a crown in Trevor's eyes.

He waited until she was halfway down the stairs before he said, "Wow. You're beautiful."

Her cheeks grew rosy. "Thank you."

Why hadn't he asked her out before tonight? Why had it taken her own father to get the ball rolling? He knew the answer, of course. He'd been trying to avoid falling for her. He wasn't trying to avoid it any longer. It was a done deal.

She reached the bottom of the stairs. "You look rather handsome yourself."

Behind Trevor, Rodney cleared his throat. "You two better get a move on. Don't want to lose your reservation at the only restaurant in town."

Trevor turned around and found Rodney holding up his daughter's coat for her. She walked to him, turned, and slipped her arms into the sleeves. Then she faced him again and kissed his cheek.

"Love you, Dad. We won't be late."

"You stay out just as long as you please.

I'm going to watch a documentary and then go to bed."

"Aren't you going to see in the New Year?"

Rodney laughed as he touched Penny's cheek. "For a man my age, a good night's sleep is more important." He took a couple of steps backward, stopping in the entrance to the living room.

Taking his cue, Trevor moved up to Penny's side. "Are you ready?"

"Yes." She smiled up at him. "I'm ready."

Penny had always thought the butterflies-in-the-stomach sensation was a myth dreamed up by the hopeless romantics. But as Trevor escorted her along the path from the porch to his truck, she discovered how real the feeling could be.

After helping her in on the passenger side, Trevor got in behind the wheel and started the engine. Then he glanced her way and smiled. "I'm glad you agreed to do this, Penny."

"Me too."

Neither of them spoke again until they reached the edge of town.

As Trevor slowed the truck to twenty miles per hour, he said, "I'll be helping take down the Christmas lights when I go to work on

Monday. Too bad. I like Main Street this way."

For some reason, the comment calmed those silly butterflies, and Penny was able to smile again. "I've often wished they'd leave the lights up year-round."

"I suppose the town council wouldn't like the power bill."

"I suppose not."

Most of the businesses in town had long since closed down, but the parking lot of the Dusty Trail Saloon had a half dozen trucks and cars in it. The Merc was still doing business too. However, it was soon apparent that the place to be in Kings Meadow tonight was the Tamarack Grill. The parking lot was full. Piles of snow, pushed aside by snowplows in recent weeks, had formed a once-white wall opposite the restaurant.

"Is it like this every year?" Trevor asked.

"To tell you the truth, I don't know. I've never come here for dinner on New Year's Eve."

Finding a place to park a fair distance from the Tamarack, he pulled his truck to the side of the road and turned the key. The night fell like a silent blanket around them. Trevor got out and came around to open her door, the snow several inches deep beneath his boots. His gaze dropped to the open-toed heels she wore.

"Not exactly snowshoes," he said as his gaze lifted to meet hers.

"I should have thought. It wasn't like this at home." She swiveled on the seat to face him. "It isn't all that far. I'll just take off my shoes and make a run for it. My feet won't freeze."

"I have a better idea."

Before she knew what was happening, she was out of the cab and held in his arms. He closed the truck door with his shoulder, then carried her across the street and up to the entrance of the restaurant. Once there he lowered her feet to the ground.

She could hardly breathe. Her heart pounded erratically and her legs felt unsteady beneath her. She feared someone might have seen him carrying her like that — almost like a bride across a threshold. At the same time she wished he held her still.

"There," he said, smiling. "That's better than running barefoot through the snow."

He was right. It was better. Much better.

He opened the door and motioned for her to enter. She complied, stopping when they reached the sign that asked them to wait to be seated. Noticeably warmer air swirled around her legs and feet.

"Here," he said. "Let me take your coat."

By the time Trevor was holding both of their coats over one arm, Cynthia Rogers, one of Tamarack's waitresses, approached them, menus at ready, a smile on her lips. "Hi, Penny." Her gaze shifted to Trevor. "Welcome back."

He answered, "Thanks. We've got a reservation. It's under Reynolds. Trevor Reynolds."

Cynthia glanced down at the open book on the hostess stand. "Yes, right this way."

Trevor placed the fingertips of one hand against the small of Penny's back and fell in slightly behind her as they followed the waitress to their table. The touch through the chiffon fabric — intimate and warm — made her skin tingle. Cynthia placed the menus on a table and stepped out of the way as Trevor held a chair for Penny. After she was seated, he put their coats on an empty third chair opposite her and took the chair to her right. Close enough for him to lean over and talk to her if he wanted.

The butterflies stirred to life again.

Cynthia told them the night's specials, then took their drink orders and left.

"They've added a few tables since the last time I was in here." Trevor removed his hat and set it on top of their coats. Music began wafting through the restaurant, drawing his gaze to a corner near the bar. "And live music too."

Penny looked in the same direction. There was a man on a keyboard, another with a guitar, and a woman on vocals. "That's a first, as far as I know. Must be something they do for New Year's."

"She's got a nice voice." His appreciation was obvious.

"Nowhere near as nice as yours." Before the words were out of her mouth, she wished them back. She didn't know why. She supposed because, for the most part, they had avoided talking about his music career. Had that been his choice or hers?

"Miss Cartwright, did you pay me a compliment?"

She looked at him again, feeling the heat rise in her cheeks. "I guess I did."

"Well, I thank you."

Cynthia returned to their table with their beverages. "Are you ready to order or do you need a little more time?"

"I know what I want," Trevor said. "Penny?"

She nodded. "I'd like one of the specials. The New Orleans barbecued shrimp and Cornish game hen."

"Sounds good. I'll have the same." Trevor took Penny's menu, then handed both menus to the waitress. After Cynthia walked away in the direction of the kitchens, he looked around the room. "Lots of familiar faces here tonight." He waved and smiled at someone.

Penny leaned to one side to see who it was. Buck and Charity Malone were seated several tables over. Charity mouthed *Hello* to Penny and waved. Penny acknowledged the silent greeting.

When she returned her gaze to Trevor, she found him watching her as if looking for an answer to some unspoken question. "What?" she said after a lengthy silence.

"Nothing. I was just thinking what a great day this has been. First our horseback ride. Now this dinner."

Pleasure coursed through her. "We haven't eaten yet. You don't know dinner will be great."

"Sure I do. I've heard great things about the chef. As you'll recall, I've met him." He leaned toward her. "Besides, it's the company that makes the evening great, much more than the food." An admiring look filled his eyes.

When he'd first seen her tonight, he'd called her beautiful. Suddenly she felt beautiful, both inside and out. No man had ever made her feel this way before.

What's happening between us? she wondered, hoping that whatever it was, it wouldn't stop.

BRAD

2014

From: Brad Cartwright
Subject: Will arrive in Nashville late
 December/early January
Date: October 7, 2014 at 9:52:24 AM
 MDT
To: Trevor Reynolds

Thanks, Trevor, for your recent e-mail.
Yes, I am definitely graduating one
semester early. Those summer classes I
took are finally paying off. I plan to
spend Christmas with my dad and sister.
Then I'll pack up my truck and head for
Nashville.

I couldn't believe it when you wrote
that your drummer is leaving the band
at the end of the year. No, I can believe
it. I've felt like God's been in charge of
this dream of mine all along.

You bet I want to audition for you. I
know I'll only get the job if I'm the best

one for it. No worries there. And no matter what happens, it's good to know I've got a friend in Nashville already. That means a lot.

Brad

CHAPTER 19

Trevor had never enjoyed looking at a woman as much as he enjoyed looking at Penny throughout dinner. Her hair. Her eyes. Her mouth and her smile. Sure, he'd always thought her pretty, but this was more than that. Then there was the sound of her voice and the melody of her laughter. They talked of many things, and no matter what she said, it seemed brilliant or interesting. The food, as he'd predicted, was delicious, made more so because of her presence.

But the evening became sheer perfection when couples began dancing to the music of the trio. Trevor hadn't noticed the space that had been left for a dance floor until couples made their way there.

"Let's join them for the next song, Miss Cartwright."

After a moment's hesitation, she nodded.

He rose and held out his hand to her. She placed her fingertips in his open palm, and he closed his hand around hers. Slowly, he drew her up from the chair and led her to the dance floor. Once there, he drew her into his arms.

The next song began. An old Anne Murray tune, "Could I Have This Dance?" He couldn't have chosen a better one for this moment. As they moved in time to the music, Trevor wondered if she heard the lyrics in her head the way he did. Did she feel them the way he did? Were they personal to her the way he wanted them to be? Could she hear him asking her the same question?

Earlier today, he'd told her he wouldn't ever marry, but tonight the thought of being without her by his side, in his arms, was almost too much to bear. Little by little over the past weeks, he'd fallen in love with her. Maybe, because of Brad, he'd already been half in love with her before he came to Kings Meadow. But even if not, he loved her now. There was no escaping that truth. He didn't want to escape it, and what surprised him most was that he wasn't surprised by the discovery any longer. He'd run from love, from commitment, because of his father, because he never wanted to make the same kind of mistakes. But Penny was right. He didn't have to repeat them. He was finished running.

Maybe this was what Brad had had in mind when he asked Trevor to come here. He'd like to think so, anyway. Maybe it was what God had had in mind too. Maybe all the resistance had been in Trevor's own head and heart. Maybe he'd just been afraid of loving someone and of being loved in return.

He lightly pressed his cheek against the top of Penny's head and breathed in the faint floral scent of her shampoo, felt the silkiness of her hair on his skin. And suddenly he wished the Tamarack Grill wasn't the best place to be this New Year's Eve. Because he wanted to kiss her, and he couldn't do that with half of Kings Meadow watching them.

At least it feels like half the town.

The song ended. Reluctantly, he loosened his hold, but he couldn't make himself take a step back from her. Several heartbeats passed, and then she was the one to put a little distance between them. But when he looked at her, she smiled. Not a wide, laughing smile. Small and almost secretive.

The desire to kiss her grew stronger.

"Hey, folks," came a male voice through the speakers. "I've had a special request for Trevor Reynolds to come up here and sing us a song or two. For those of you who might not know, Trevor's come to us from Nashville, where he's a singer. Our own Brad Cartwright was the drummer in his band."

The intimate moment was shattered into a thousand pieces. Trevor's gaze snapped toward the trio. Would hearing her brother's name bring hurt back into Penny's eyes? Would his singing make the memory worse? He didn't want to do that to her. Not now.

A smattering of applause began, encouraging him to go to the microphone.

"Go ahead, Trevor," someone called from the far side of the restaurant. "Sing 'Keeper of the Stars.' "

More applause, louder this time.

His gaze swung back to Penny. He'd expected thoughts of Brad to erase her smile — like they had the night they went caroling — but it was still there, although muted.

"Go ahead, Trevor," she echoed softly. "Everyone wants to hear you sing."

"You're sure?"

She nodded. "I'm sure."

"Penny," a woman said from a nearby table, "come and join us."

She looked, nodded again, and allowed Trevor to escort her to the empty chair. He didn't recognize the couple at the table, and she didn't perform introductions.

He leaned down, his mouth near her ear. "I won't be long." When he straightened, he saw the soft smile remained. He took encouragement from it as he made his way toward the microphone, his steps unhurried and measured. It wasn't stage fright he felt. Performing better than two hundred days per year for the last decade in all kinds of circumstances had stripped him of most of his performance nerves.

He reached the makeshift stage and took the proffered microphone in his right hand. "Thanks." His gaze swept the restaurant.

Conversations had died by this time. There was only the occasional clink of table service against dinnerware and some muffled sounds from the kitchen. As he'd noted earlier, he was no longer an unfamiliar face among strangers. He'd been introduced to many of them since the day of his arrival. He'd been made a part of this community. When was the last time he'd felt that way? Had he ever?

"Sing 'Keeper of the Stars,' " came that same male voice. Trevor was tempted to shade his eyes and discover who it was. Instead he turned toward the two men behind him. They nodded, understanding the unspoken question. They knew the song. He told them what key he wanted and then turned back to his audience.

After Trevor's return to Nashville following Brad's funeral and Trevor's visit to his mom's, he and his remaining band members had tried to fulfill their touring commitments. They'd hired another drummer and gone back on the road. But Trevor's heart hadn't been in the music. He hadn't wanted to entertain anyone, hadn't wanted to perform, hadn't wanted to even sing in the shower. In under a week he'd known what he had to do: cancel all remaining engagements and disband while he took the time to grieve the death of his friend. He and the boys had all said it was temporary, that they would be back together again in time. But so much had changed since then — both circumstances and Trevor himself. Did he even want to go back to the old way of living?

Lifting the mic to his mouth, he repeated, "Thanks," then gave a nod of his head.

The keyboardist was accomplished. It sounded as if someone played a violin, the way Trevor had recorded the song for his one and only album.

"It was no accident . . ." As natural as breathing, he sang, his gaze moving to Penny and remaining there, wanting her to know he believed the words of the song, hoping he wasn't moving too fast.

Penny was mesmerized.

"Long before we ever knew . . . ," Trevor crooned in that smooth voice of his.

She was captivated. By the look in his eyes. By the words of the song that he seemed to sing straight to her. Was that possible? And even if he did mean them, what could the future hold for a small-town librarian and a traveling musician? He'd said himself, this very day, that marriage wasn't something he wanted. Would that change in the future? Had that changed in only a few hours?

The requested song was the same one that had caused an unexpected longing for romantic love to well up inside of Penny. Perhaps that's all she felt now. Just a wish for something she didn't have. Just sentimentality because of a popular love song. Maybe it had nothing to do with the man who sang the words.

Or maybe it had everything to do with him.

She tried to draw in a deep breath, but there was no steadying the rapid beat of her heart. There were dozens of reasons why it would be foolish to care for him — to love him — more than she already did.

It's okay for you to be happy.

It didn't seem like an important thought at first. But then, despite all the distractions in the restaurant, she realized God had spoken an important truth into her spirit. In an instant she understood that she'd allowed herself to believe she didn't deserve to live fully, to be happy, that she felt guilty for being alive and having a future. Her brother's life had ended, and she'd expected to pay a penalty for continuing to live on. How had her thinking become so twisted?

Perhaps, she answered, *because I blamed You even more than I blamed Trevor.*

And with that admission came peace. In a breath, she felt the balm of God's forgiveness wash over her heart and a feeling of freedom replace the knot of fear that had resided inside of her for such a long, long time. She felt free. Free to live. Free to love.

The song ended and applause erupted throughout the restaurant. Trevor smiled as his gaze finally left Penny and slowly moved over the audience.

"Thanks, everyone." He turned and handed the microphone back to the vocalist. Someone called for another song, but Trevor shook his head before walking to where Penny sat. "Maybe we should go."

She nodded, understanding. If they stayed,

someone would always be watching them or asking Trevor for an autograph or for one more song. She took his hand and he drew her to her feet. They nodded at the couple — Ashley Holloway and her husband, Vic — who had welcomed Penny to their table but to whom she hadn't spoken anything beyond, "Hi."

The trio began playing again. Couples returned to the dance floor. Trevor and Penny went against the tide as they made their way to their table. They collected their coats, his hat, and her clutch. A short while later they stood outside the entrance.

Trevor glanced down at her feet, then up at her eyes. "Ready?"

She suddenly felt giddy, as if she'd been drinking champagne with her dinner instead of iced tea.

As before, he swept her off her feet as if she were as light as a feather. And why did this journey across the snow-covered street seem much too short, unlike when he'd carried her the opposite direction? With surprising ease, he unlocked the truck and opened the passenger door while still holding her in his arms. Then he set her on the seat, his hands lingering on her waist.

Would he kiss her? She wanted him to kiss her. Could he see it in her eyes? *Please see it in my eyes.*

There was a breathless moment when he drew closer to her, and she was certain she was about to get her wish. Then a car rounded a bend in the road. Headlights bathed Trevor in a yellow-white flash. Only for a few seconds before the automobile rolled past them and darkness returned. But the brightness of the lights had been enough to break the spell. He stepped back, gave her an apologetic smile — at least, that was what it seemed to her — and closed the door.

The drive home was made in silence, and Penny wished she could read his thoughts. Maybe he hadn't been close to kissing her. Maybe she'd only imagined it. Maybe she'd imagined everything. What did she know? She'd never been in love before, and no man had ever been in love with her. Not really in love.

When they got to the ranch, Trevor walked with her along the cleared path to the porch steps.

"Would you like to come in?" she asked as they climbed the steps. "It isn't New Year's yet. I can make us some decaf while we wait for midnight."

"Sure. I'll come in."

Penny tried the door. It was unlocked. Her

dad had always left the door unlocked for her when she was on a date, even after she was older and he no longer waited up for her. A lamp had been left on in the living room, but the rest of the house was dark and quiet.

She put her small clutch on the entry table, and without a word Trevor helped her out of her coat. He placed his hat next to her purse. His coat covered hers on the coat tree. Then he followed her into the kitchen. He didn't take a seat at the table, as expected. Instead, he stood only a few feet away from the coffeemaker, observing her every movement. She felt nervous and clumsy.

"You know," he said, his voice low, "maybe coffee isn't what I want."

Two steps was all it took for him to be at her side. Two short steps. With a gentle but firm grip on her shoulders, he turned her to face him. She lost the ability to breathe as he placed an index finger under her chin and tilted her face up so that their gazes met.

"Penny . . ."

He spoke her name so softly she wasn't sure he'd said anything at all. But by then he was kissing her, and she no longer cared what had or had not been said.

CHAPTER 20

Wearing a pair of comfortable jeans and a bulky blue-and-white sweater, Penny hummed to herself as she descended the stairs early the next morning. Her father was seated at the kitchen table, reading the newspaper on his iPad while drinking coffee. Fred and Ginger lay beneath the table, heads on paws.

Her dad looked at her and immediately put down the iPad. "You're up mighty early. I take it you had a good time last night."

"Mmm." Her smile widened. She couldn't help it. "A very good time."

"I'm glad."

She poured herself a cup of coffee. "Me too."

"Any plans for today?"

"Yes." She turned and leaned her backside against the counter. "Trevor and I are driving down to Boise for the day. We thought we'd go to the mall and maybe take in a movie and whatever else suits our fancy. He said he would arrange for friends to take care of the livestock without him today, so you don't have to worry about that."

"I wasn't worried."

"Dad?"

"Hmm?"

"I really like Trevor." *Really, really like him.* "I was wrong about him. In lots of ways."

Her dad looked at her in silence for a long time, then nodded.

"I never expected to feel this way."

"Life often takes us by surprise, my girl."

Penny gazed into her mug. She'd never been big on surprises, but she rather liked this one.

Ginger whimpered and got to her feet, her ears cocked forward. Fred followed a moment later. Then both dogs dashed out of the kitchen, through the mudroom, and outside through the pet door. Penny's pulse quickened as if she too had heard the arrival of Trevor's truck.

"Must be him now," her dad said, needlessly.

She put down her mug and headed for the front door. When she opened it, Trevor was already out of the cab and giving each of the dogs the attention their exuberant welcome deserved.

He straightened, saw her, and smiled. "Morning."

"Good morning."

Another truck rolled into the barnyard, two men in the cab.

Trevor said, "Looks like the first shift is here."

Penny said a silent word of thanks to God for the way their neighbors continued to pitch in to help her dad. Over the years, she'd seen the people of this valley do the same for other folks, time and again. She — and her mother before her — had prepared casseroles and individual frozen meals whenever word went out about someone in need.

While Trevor went over to speak to Chet and Grant, Penny gave the men a wave and retreated into the house. She entered the kitchen moments later. "Dad, shall I fix your breakfast before we go?"

"No, thank you. Unless you two plan to eat with me before you go."

She shook her head. "We're going to enjoy a New Year's brunch at some restaurant in Boise. Trevor's got that planned too."

"Full of plans, that boy." He chuckled softly.

Her dad was amused by his own comment, but it troubled Penny. Perhaps because she had no idea where those plans of Trevor's were headed. Not today, but further down the road. He hadn't said he loved her. She hadn't said she loved him. But if they were in love, where would it lead?

As clear as if she were at the Tamarack again, she heard him singing in her memory. He had an amazing voice, an amazing stage presence. And he had a smile that could melt women's hearts. He could be a star. He *should* be a star.

But where does that leave me? There's Dad and this ranch and my job. What about —

Penny closed her eyes and determinedly drove such thoughts from her mind. She would not let the uncertainty of tomorrow spoil the joy of today. For once, she didn't have to map out the future step by step. She didn't have to be in absolute total control. She could live in the moment instead.

A whisper of cold air told her a door had opened and Trevor had entered the house. After a bit of foot stomping to make certain no snow was left on his boots, he strode into the kitchen.

"Morning," he said to her again. Then to her dad, "Good morning, sir."

"Morning, Trevor. Penny tells me you have a full day of fun planned down in the valley."

305

"We do." Trevor glanced back at Penny. "Well, I hope it'll be fun anyway."

She remembered his kisses. They'd stood in almost this very same spot. Her stomach tumbled and her cheeks grew warm.

"Are you ready?" He smiled as if he'd read her thoughts.

"Just let me get my purse from the bedroom." She spun around and hurried up the stairs.

Rodney was neither blind nor stupid. His daughter more than *liked* Trevor Reynolds. And unless Rodney's eyes deceived him, the young man felt very much the same way about Penny. If he'd been alone in the kitchen, he might have done a little jig of joy. Instead he lifted the iPad and feigned renewed interest in the *Idaho Statesman*.

"Sir?" Trevor crossed to the table. "Did you think about my offer? Of a loan?"

"I have." In truth, he'd thought about the offer many times since it had been made. He'd thought about it and rejected it again and again.

Trevor raised his eyebrows, urging more of an answer.

Rodney shook his head. "I don't believe it would be wise to accept. You could loan the money to me, and the ranch could still not do well enough to survive. You could lose your savings, and I would have no way to repay you. I'm not a young man nor a completely healthy one."

"I'm not worried about losing the money."

"You should be."

They both heard hurried footsteps on the stairs.

Trevor offered a brief smile as he took a step back from the table. "Keep thinking about it, sir. I'll be asking you to reconsider next time we talk."

If nothing else, Trevor was a tenacious young man.

Rodney nodded just before his daughter reentered the kitchen.

It was an easy drive down to Boise. Except for places where steep mountainsides kept the road in shadows, the highway was clear of snow and ice. There was little other traffic to contend with at this hour on New Year's Day. Trevor supposed most travelers were already at their destinations for the first full day of a long weekend. While still passing through the foothills, they dropped below the snow line. And once they reached the valley floor, there wasn't a hint of white remaining.

"Where exactly are we going for brunch?"

Penny asked, breaking the most recent silence.

"You'll see." He pulled his phone from his shirt pocket and handed it to her. "Tap the icon that says Maps. All you should have to do then is tap Start, and it'll give us directions. I've got it all set up."

She laughed softly as she looked at the phone's screen. "I've forgotten what this is like."

"What what's like?"

"I haven't had a cell phone since I finished grad school. It isn't worth the cost for the rare times I could use it. I'm not in range of a tower often enough to justify the expense."

Just then, a male voice from the phone advised Trevor that his next turn was up ahead.

Penny laughed. "My last cell phone definitely didn't talk to me."

"I have to admit, I found it disorienting when I got to Kings Meadow and my phone became basically useless. You know, not being able to check my e-mails and go on the Internet whenever I wanted to look something up." He shrugged. "But I've gotten used to it." He hesitated a moment, then added, "It's not all that bad to be disconnected from 24/7 social media and e-mail."

From the corner of his eye, he saw Penny

turn her gaze in his direction, perhaps studying him to ascertain if he'd spoken the truth. He hoped she would see the answer. He hoped she would discover many truths about him during this day.

The restaurant where they had brunch was the perfect setting. Relaxed enough that they didn't feel underdressed in Levis and boots. Fancy enough that they felt like they were dining someplace out of the ordinary. They talked some, ate a little more, and gazed into each other's eyes. Often — perhaps too often — Trevor was tempted to declare his love to her, to speak the words aloud for the first time. But something held him back. He had to find the perfect moment.

After finishing brunch, Trevor followed his phone's GPS to their next destination, one he hadn't mentioned to Penny in advance.

"What are we doing here?" she asked as she stared up at the sign on the amusement center's building.

"We're going to race go-carts."

"We're going to what?"

"Race go-carts."

She gave him a look that said she thought he was crazy.

"Come on. You spend all of your working hours shut up in a library. Yesterday you admitted it was ages since you'd had time to go horseback riding."

Last summer, on a particularly long drive from one venue to another, Brad had shared more stories about his boyhood and especially about the sister he adored. Despite the difference in their ages, they'd been close and had taken part in many an escapade. The picture of Penny that Trevor had formed in his mind as Brad talked that night was very much like the woman he saw now — teasing, laughing, fun loving. Quite different from the serious, worried, heartbroken woman he'd met upon arriving in Idaho.

Trevor continued, "You need to let your hair down, as they say. Have a bit of fun. The way you used to when you were a kid."

"I have been having fun. I *am* having fun."

Her smile made him feel like a million bucks.

She reached for the door handle. "Well, let's get going. I want to beat you around the track before it's time to see that movie you promised me." With that, she opened the truck door and dropped to the ground.

"Beat me?" He laughed as he hurried to follow after her. "Who said you were going to beat me?"

"*I* did!"

Trevor wasn't the sort of guy to lose a challenge on purpose, but he might have done so for Penny . . . if she'd needed him to. She didn't. She drove with wild abandon, coming in first more than once.

From the amusement center they headed to the theater to see one of the recent holiday season's box-office hits. Because the movie had been playing since Thanksgiving, Trevor and Penny had the theater mostly to themselves. While they watched the movie, they snacked on buttered popcorn and sodas.

From the theater complex, they headed to the mall to check out sales, although neither of them seemed inclined to buy anything. Both were satisfied with looking and showing the other what they'd found, from watches to snow boots, from funky scarves to diamond bracelets. But they had the most fun in the as-advertised-on-TV aisle of one department store. With one gadget after another, they made up outlandish advertising slogans for the products they found on the shelves. Perhaps other customers found their antics irritating, but Trevor and Penny were completely entertained by their own silliness.

Sides aching from laughter, they walked to the food court, where they got their choice of fast food to eat before their drive back to Kings Meadow. Finding an empty table surrounded by other empty tables, they sat down.

Penny slid her burrito up from the paper that held it. "Thank you for today, Trevor. It really was the most fun I've had in ages."

"I feel the same way." *More than that. I love you, Penny.* But now still wasn't the right time.

His cell phone rang, causing them both to startle at the unexpected sound. Trevor chuckled as he withdrew the phone from his shirt pocket. The caller ID told him it was Beck Thompson. He mouthed the word *Sorry* to Penny, then punched the button to answer the call. "Hey, Beck. Didn't expect to hear from you again this soon."

"And I didn't expect you to pick up. But I'm sure glad you did 'cause I've got big news."

Although she couldn't hear the other side of the conversation, Trevor rolled his eyes at Penny.

"Trev, that producer I told you about? I saw him again and gave him your CD. He listened to it and likes your sound. He wants to meet with you. I really think there's a

312

chance you could get signed to a major recording label."

"You're kidding."

"I'm dead serious. So how soon can you get here?"

Trevor looked across the table once more. Penny was eating her burrito, gaze fastened on her tray, but he knew she listened to his side of the conversation. "I'll have to think about it, Beck. See what I can arrange. I'll call you back in a few days. All right?"

"Sure. Fine by me. I did think you'd be a little more jacked about it. All I can say is don't let this chance pass you by. It could be the big break you've been waiting for all these years."

"Yeah, I understand. I'll talk to you soon. Thanks. I mean it."

"Sure thing. Later."

Trevor pressed the End button. A chance. A real chance of hitting it big. It was what he'd wanted for nearly as long as he could remember. But it would mean leaving Idaho . . .

And Penny.

BRAD
2015

Brad and Trevor walked out of the truck stop a little before midnight. The September night was still warm, more like summer than early autumn.

"You sure you want to drive, Brad?"

"I'm sure. I'm good for another hour or two at least."

"Well, I'm beat. I'm getting in the back and grabbing some shut-eye. You're sure you're good? 'Cause we can find a motel if you want."

Brad gave his friend a shove on the arm, repeating, "I'm sure I'm good."

What he didn't tell Trevor was that he'd felt compelled throughout the day to be in prayer. He'd prayed in spurts between conversations in the daylight hours, but it would be easier with Trevor asleep in the backseat.

Since God hadn't told him exactly who or what needed to be covered in prayer, Brad

worked his way through a familiar list —
praying for his dad's health; praying that
Penny would finally get over her anger, that
she would finally forgive him for leaving
Idaho; praying for his trip home for Thanksgiving; praying for Trevor to know the Mes-
siah, that his heart would be healed and he
would experience new life.

*He's so close, Lord. And I keep feeling like
something's going to happen when we get to
Kings Meadow in a couple of months, that
You've prepared something special for him
there. I don't know what it is, but I believe that
something's going to happen.*

As he continued to pray, miles and miles
of highway rolled away, the moonless night
and the rural landscape as dark as pitch.
Sometimes it felt like only he and God
existed in all the universe, just the two of
them, talking about life and love. He felt his
heart well up with joy, with praise, with a
sense of anticipation unlike anything he'd
ever felt before.

He didn't even know when his eyes began
to grow heavy.

Jesus.

CHAPTER 21

Late on Monday afternoon, three days after her New Year's excursion with Trevor, Penny stood at the large glass windows looking out on the library parking lot. Darkness had already fallen over Kings Meadow, and for some reason, the hush in the building felt . . . ominous.

"That's silly," she muttered.

Maybe if she could stop thinking about Trevor, she wouldn't be in this strange mood. They'd had such a wonderful time together in Boise. Every moment had seemed perfection. Right up until they left the mall for the drive home. By then Trevor had seemed . . . different. He'd pulled away from her in a way she couldn't quite define.

And other than when he was tending to the livestock, he hadn't spent time at the ranch. He hadn't been unfriendly or discourteous. Just withdrawn. Distracted. Never completely engaged in any conversation she'd had with him.

Better not to let yourself care so much.

That advice was as easy to follow as telling herself not to breathe as much.

Because I love him. Completely, thoroughly love him.

How had she allowed that to happen? Shouldn't she have known that not following a plan, that living in the moment, would end with heartbreak?

"Miss Cartwright?"

The soft female voice surprised Penny from her thoughts. She turned around to find Sharon Malone — the middle daughter of the high school principal — standing nearby, a slip of yellow scratch paper in her hand.

The girl held it toward her. "I can't find this book on the shelf. Is it checked out?"

"Let's see, shall we?" Glad for something to do, welcoming any diversion, Penny walked to the computer behind the library checkout counter. In moments, she knew the desired book should be on the shelf. She jotted down the call number. "It's in the library, Sharon. Maybe someone used it and then put it back in the wrong place. That happens."

For the next fifteen minutes or so, Penny and Sharon searched the library stacks for the missing book. By the time the book was found, Sharon's dad, Ken, had arrived to take her home.

"I just need to check this book out, Dad," the girl called to him in a stage whisper.

"Okay." He waved at Penny. "No rush."

Penny waved back as she took both book and library card from Sharon. When the checkout was finished, Sharon stuffed the book into her backpack, adding it to at least four or five large school textbooks. Then she slung the bag over one shoulder and hurried toward her dad.

A few minutes later, the front doors closed behind the last library patron, and Penny was able to begin locking up and shutting down for the night. But with the silence came thoughts of Trevor again. Would he still be at the ranch when she got home or would he have departed already? Would they have a chance to talk? Would he tell her what troubled him?

The last of her tasks accomplished, Penny went to the back room and put on her warm winter outerwear. She glanced over her shoulder, hoping she hadn't forgotten anything while thinking about Trevor. Then with a sigh, she went out into the cold, dark evening, locking the dead bolt behind her.

The smell of snow was in the air, and it

didn't please her to think of it. She'd welcomed those first snowfalls of the season, as she did every year. Now she dreaded the thought of more snow. She was tired of white. Even more tired of piles of dirty snow pushed to the sides of the roads and parking lots. She had a sudden and fierce longing for spring, for new life and fresh beginnings. She was tired of dark and dormant.

She got into her car and started the engine, then pressed her forehead against the cold steering wheel. "God, I feel so lost right now. I shouldn't. I know I shouldn't. But I do. And I'm afraid. I'm afraid because I let myself care for Trevor, and now . . . now . . . What if he can't love me in return?"

Trevor finished mucking out the stall and put fresh feed in the manger. A short while later, he returned Harmony to the enclosure, where she promptly plunged her muzzle into the fragrant alfalfa hay. Crunching sounds broke the silence of the barn.

"You've had something weighing on your mind these past few days," Rodney said from near the front entrance.

Trevor turned. "I didn't know you were still out here, sir."

The older man moved toward him, his expression thoughtful, his steps unhurried.

"Is it something you don't want to talk about? You can tell me if it's none of my business."

"No." He shook his head. "It's not that. It's that I don't know *how* to talk about it." He leaned his back against the stall railings.

Rodney sat on a wooden stool not far away. He crossed his arms over his chest, saying without words that he could be patient.

Trevor released a sigh as he sank onto a storage bin. "You know, I can't remember a time when my father was willing to sit, like you are now, and listen to anything I had to say. Most of the time when we were together or when we talked on the phone, he just let me know what a disappointment I was as a son."

"I'm sorry, Trevor. Very sorry. I'm sure that wasn't easy for you."

He didn't know why he'd brought up his dad. That wasn't what had been weighing on his mind, as Rodney had put it. It was something else entirely. Ever since Beck's call, he'd been trying to figure out what he wanted to do with his music. What he *should* do. A few months ago, maybe even a few weeks ago, he wouldn't have wondered for a second. He would have known in a heartbeat. He'd always wanted fame and fortune.

Wanted it more than anything else. He'd wanted to be one of those grinning singers who ran up onto the stage to receive an award. He'd wanted to rub shoulders as an equal with the greats of country music. All the greats. From those who'd been playing and singing for fifty years to teenagers who'd recently burst onto the scene. But now —

"Tell me more about your father," Rodney prompted gently.

Trevor shrugged. "He didn't have much kindness in him. Not toward anybody. Including Mom." He drew in a long, slow breath and released it. "I've tried to forgive him for the way he was, but it's been hard."

Rodney scratched his head with an index finger. "Life is messy. And like they say, 'Hurting people hurt people.' From the little Dot told me about your father, I'm guessing he was full of hurt."

His dad full of hurt? Yeah, Trevor supposed that was true. His dad had been raised by a widowed father on a farm on the prairies of North Dakota. Judging by the few photographs Trevor had seen, they'd lived in extreme poverty. His father had fought hard to be allowed to complete high school, even though Trevor's grandfather wanted him working the farm. And he'd taken on two jobs to put himself through college. Once married, he'd provided well financially for his wife and son, despite the way he wielded words to wound those nearest to him.

"I guess he did the best he could," Trevor said, more to himself than to Rodney.

"That's how we go through life. Just doing the best we can do at the time. Perhaps tomorrow we'll be able to do better. But for today, we do the best we can. And along the way we try to get the log out of our own eye before we help someone take the speck out of theirs."

"Something Jesus said. Right?"

"Yes."

Trevor stared at a piece of straw, rolling it between thumb and index finger.

"Mind if I tell you a story?"

"Of course not." He looked up. The only light in the barn came from a lantern sitting on the workbench behind Rodney, which kept the older man's face in shadows.

"When I was a little kid, maybe five years old, my mom and I went to a carnival. Or maybe it was the fair. Anyway, somebody gave me a bunch of helium-filled balloons. I about got a crick in my neck, bending my head back so I could look up at them." He chuckled softly. "Well, it got real crowded all of a sudden. I got jostled between folks and separated from my mom. It scared me so much I let go of all of those strings."

Trevor had played enough fairs to imagine the scene.

"That bouquet of balloons floated away. They went higher and higher. And you know what? I liked the look of them more from a distance."

Trevor knew the older man watched him, although he couldn't see the expression in his eyes.

"It's like that with a lot of the things we hold on to, son. Good and bad. We grip those strings tight, not wanting to ever let go. They're ours and we want to hang on. We don't want to let go of the things or the people we love and we don't want to let go of the pain others cause us. Not by accident and not on purpose. Because they're familiar, I guess. But the truth is, letting go gives us freedom to see what we've released from a whole new perspective."

Funny, the effect Rodney's words had on him. It was as if he was that kid at the fair, but instead of a bunch of balloons, his strings were tied to the hurt and resentment he felt whenever he thought of his father. He stared at those imaginary strings while pondering Rodney's words, letting them sink in. And finally, as he sat there in the dim light of the barn, he felt himself let go of those strings. Through the eyes of his new faith, he watched them float away.

I forgive you, Dad. I really do forgive you.

It was going to be okay. *He* was going to be okay.

"Thanks," he said after a long while.

Rodney nodded. "Don't know why I even thought of that story. Just seemed like the thing to tell you." He cleared his throat. "But I feel like there's something else troubling you. Am I wrong?"

Trevor almost shook his head, almost confessed the confusion he'd wrestled with since Beck's second phone call, almost explained the decision he needed to make. But then he realized his confusion was gone. He was at peace with more than just the memories of his father. And it wasn't Rodney he needed to talk to about it anyway.

CHAPTER 22

Disappointment stung Penny's heart as her headlights swept across the barnyard. Trevor's truck wasn't there. He hadn't waited for her, hadn't delayed his departure. She'd hoped —

Well, it didn't matter what she'd hoped.

It is what it is. I'll get over him. He won't be around forever.

She parked her car in the garage and hurried toward the entrance to the mudroom. Snowflakes landed on her nose and cheeks before she reached the door.

"Hey, Dad," she called as she shrugged out of her coat. "I'm home."

She walked into the kitchen, expecting to find her dad standing near the stove as he usually did on the nights when she worked until closing. But he wasn't there. In fact, there were no signs of dinner preparation.

"Dad?"

"I'm in the living room."

Her heart fluttered in fear. Was something wrong? Was he sick? Was he hurt? But when she reached the living room, she found him in his favorite chair, a book open in his lap, the twenty-four-hour news station playing softly on the television.

"Hi, hon. Did you have a good day?"

"It was all right." She glanced over her shoulder toward the kitchen.

"I didn't cook tonight. Trevor said he would grab burgers, fries, and milk shakes on his way back from town."

Her heart fluttered again, but the sensation was different this time. "He's coming back tonight?"

"Hmm." Her dad nodded. "He said he needs to talk to you about something."

She'd wanted Trevor to talk to her. About anything. Only now she wasn't sure she was ready to hear whatever it was he had to say. Trying to sound calm, she said, "I'm going to change my clothes."

Once out of her dad's sight, she hurried up the stairs to her bedroom, where she shed her business attire and replaced it with jeans, sweater, and her slippers. In the bathroom, she brushed her teeth before sweeping her hair into a ponytail. She paused afterward to stare at her reflection in the mirror.

"Whatever's been going on these last few days, you're about to find out." Nerves tumbled in her stomach.

A bark from one of the dogs drew her out of the bathroom to the bedroom window. She was in time to see Trevor's pickup roll to a halt near the front porch. The headlights went off. The engine died. The truck door opened, and Trevor, visible in the porch light, dropped to the ground. He looked up, perhaps at the falling snow, but it caused her to step back from the window, feeling as if she'd been caught spying. She heard the truck door close. Snow crunched. Footsteps fell on the porch below her window. A knock sounded. Silence, then she heard the men talking, although too softly for her to make out the words.

Drawing a breath for courage, she headed out of her room and down the stairs. When she entered the living room, she found Trevor standing in the center of the room, holding Tux in the crook of his arm and scratching the feline behind one ear.

Lucky cat.

He saw her, seemed to hesitate, and then smiled so briefly she almost missed it. "Are you hungry? I brought burgers and fries. And your dad said to get you a strawberry shake."

She nodded, not knowing if she answered his question or wanted to confirm the flavor of milk shake. Not that it mattered. She was too nervous to care.

Her dad rose from his chair. "I hope you young folks won't mind, but I think I'll eat here in the living room on a tray. There's a program I want to see that's about to start." He walked out of the room.

Trevor set the cat on the floor, giving the feline's sleek coat one long stroke before straightening. "I hope you don't mind that I came back this evening."

This time she shook her head.

He motioned toward the kitchen. "Maybe we'd better eat before everything gets cold."

"Okay." She turned around, and when she did, she noticed something in the entry hall. A guitar case. It had to be Trevor's, but why had he brought it here? Rather than ask the question, she led the way out of the living room, down the entry, and into the kitchen.

Her dad was setting a tall glass of water on the tray beside a tossed green salad and a baked chicken breast. When he glanced her way he said, "Your food's on the table." Then he carried the tray from the room.

Wordlessly, Penny and Trevor sat at the table, facing one another. They ate, and Penny supposed the hamburger and shake had flavor, although she didn't taste anything. They even talked a little, about things that didn't matter to either of them. Finally, unable to bear the unspoken any longer, she pushed her half-eaten meal aside.

"Why did you come back tonight, Trevor?" It wasn't exactly the question she wanted to ask, but it was a start.

He finger-combed his hair with one hand, leaving it in the disheveled state that looked so good on him. "Remember that phone call I got on my cell when we were in Boise?"

"Of course." Everything had been different after that call.

"It was a guy who used to be in my band years ago. He wants me to come back to Nashville. There's a chance — a good one, he says — that I could get a recording contract. It's what I've wanted and worked for all of these years."

Trevor's music had taken her brother away. Now it was going to take Trevor away too. She wanted to hate and despise Nashville and country music and all it represented. But she couldn't. She'd heard him sing. He deserved all the success he'd worked for. What was that old adage? If you love someone, set them free.

"But, Penny, there's something I want more than fame and fortune. I realized that tonight."

The breath caught in her lungs.

"Sure, I love to sing. I love to entertain. But these weeks in Kings Meadow, the Lord has opened my eyes to where my real treasure lies. I've got to want Him more than anything else. And if I live for Him first, if I want Him most, I just might become the kind of man you would . . . you would want to spend your life with."

Trevor watched her expression, saw her trying to find the meaning in what he'd said thus far. "Just a minute." He held his hand out, like a traffic cop. "Don't move." He got up and left the kitchen, returning as fast as he could with the guitar case in hand. He stopped at the table but didn't sit down.

More confusion filled her eyes as she looked up at him.

"I love you, Penny. I didn't know it was possible to love anybody the way I love you. Do you think you could ever learn to love me too?"

At last, the hint of a smile curved her mouth. "Oh, Trevor. I already love you."

"Then marry me."

The tiny smile vanished. "I can't. There's Dad and the ranch and my job. How could I leave —"

"I'm not asking you to leave. I'm asking you to let me stay. To let me be a part of all that you love."

"But your career." Tears welled in her eyes. "How could I take that away from you?"

He set the guitar case on the floor at her feet. "You wouldn't be taking it away from me, Penny. I'm offering it up."

"You want to give up singing?"

"Not give it up." He knelt on one knee beside the case. "But offer it up. Let God have it to do with it what He wants. Maybe He'll want me to sing worship songs for Him someday, like my mom said. Or maybe I'll just spend my life singing and writing songs to you."

She covered her mouth with the fingertips of her right hand, the tears now rolling slowly down her cheeks.

There was a verse in the Bible where God told Joshua to meditate on the law, on the Scriptures, day and night and to obey what was written there, and that if he did that, then God would prosper Joshua's way and give him success. When Trevor had first read that verse, he'd thought it meant if he straightened out his own life, if he was obedient and followed all the Christian rules, he would finally get what he'd chased after for over a decade. But now he knew the success spoken of wasn't necessarily success as the world judges it. God's kind of success was far beyond what most people coveted, and it was *that* kind of success, God's kind, he longed for now.

"Marry me, Penny. Let me feed the cows three times a day. Let me ride horses with you through the snow in the winter and through the forests in the summer. Let me see a calf being born on a cold February morning. Let me see Harmony's foal stand beside her, all legs and fuzzy coat."

"But what if —"

"Let me be a part of your life, of your dad's life, of this town's life. Let me be the man God brought me here to become."

"Trevor, I —"

He stood, reached out, and drew her into his embrace. Then he kissed her, a slow, deep kiss that tried to say everything his words could not. When their lips parted, he whispered, "I love you, Penny Cartwright. Finding you was no accident. It was meant to be."

She opened her eyes.

"God knew what He was doing when He joined our two hearts." He kissed her forehead. "Like the song says, you take my breath away." He kissed the tip of her nose.

"You know, I never understood those lyrics until I fell in love with you." He brushed his lips lightly against hers. "Marry me." Another feathery kiss. "Marry me." And when she didn't answer, one more kiss and a whispered, "Marry me."

Her tears welled again, but she smiled now. "Yes, Trevor. Yes, I'll marry you."

Later, he would be sure to thank the God who kept the stars for giving him this woman, for blessing him with all he would ever need.

For now, he meant to keep right on kissing her. And she seemed perfectly willing to let him.

Epilogue
AUGUST 20

"All right," the photographer said in a loud voice. "Look at me and smile while you pretend to cut the cake."

There was no need for the bride to be told to smile. Penny couldn't stop smiling even if she tried.

Half an hour later, the last of the photographs had been taken, and Penny and Trevor looked out from the wings of the stage, his arm around her waist. The fellowship hall of the church — filled with lifelong friends and neighbors and a few Nashville guests as well — buzzed with happy voices that rose and fell like the waves of the sea.

She saw her dad, looking handsome in his morning coat. He'd lost weight, a healthy weight loss, since improving his diet. And his new exercise routine, started because of the diabetes, had improved his back as well. Beside him — looking pretty in a lavender lace dress — was Dot Reynolds. It occurred to Penny that her dad and Dot would make a very nice couple. They were already good friends. She wondered —

"Stranger things have happened," Trevor whispered.

She laughed, loving that he'd read her thoughts. Then she allowed her gaze to roam the large room again.

She spied Grant and Skye Nichols, Skye looking ready to have her first baby any day now. Perhaps at any moment — which would certainly add a unique twist to Penny's wedding day.

Next to them were Buck and Charity Malone. Last summer, their outdoor wedding in the town park had been the biggest event Kings Meadow had ever seen. Penny had thought it lovely, of course, but her choice had been a smaller affair. Only a maid of honor and one bridesmaid. A wedding gown found on the sale rack at the bridal shop in Boise. Wildflowers for her bouquet.

Sprinkled throughout the crowd were the men who had done so much to help the Cartwrights during her dad's illness and recovery. Men like Chet Leonard, Ollie Abbott, Rand Foster, Patrick Lester, and Tom Butler. And their wives beside them, who had provided food for the family when preparing meals was the last thing anyone wanted to do.

A fresh appreciation for the people of Kings Meadow welled in her heart. She remembered once wanting to find a job outside of Idaho. Now she found it hard to imagine ever wanting to leave.

This was home. Her home. Hers and Trevor's. And someday, God willing, their children's home too. Out of the ashes of pain and anger and bitterness of a year ago had come an unexpected joy and peace and a future for her to share with Trevor.

She didn't bother to thank her lucky stars. She didn't believe in them. But she did take a moment to thank the Keeper of the stars. It was a good way to begin a marriage.

NOTE TO READERS

Dear Friends:

It wasn't easy to type "The end" on *Keeper of the Stars* because it meant saying farewell to the friends I've made in Kings Meadow. I hope you've come to love the setting and the characters as much as I have.

I keep hearing from readers, asking about the order of the stories set in Kings Meadow. It is a bit confusing since only three of the five are part of the Kings Meadow Romance series. You can, of course, find the information on my website (www.robinleehatcher.com), but I will share it here as well:

A Promise Kept (single title women's fiction)

Love Without End (Kings Meadow Romance, Book One)

Whenever You Come Around (Kings Meadow Romance, Book Two)

I Hope You Dance (a July wedding story in the Year of Weddings series)

Keeper of the Stars (Kings Meadow Romance, Book Three)

As I write this note, still many months from the release date, I haven't settled on what story I will write next. So instead of introducing you to some new characters or a new series as I often do in a note to my readers, I'll invite you to visit my website where you can always find the most up-to-date information.

If you enjoyed this book, I hope you'll take a moment to leave a review on Goodreads and/or Amazon and/or some other book retailer or review site. Those reviews are far more important than you may know and are deeply appreciated.

In the grip of His grace,
Robin

DISCUSSION QUESTIONS

1. Penny Cartwright knew some hard losses and fell into the habit of trying to control her life and the lives of those she loved. Have you ever done something similar? Were you ever truly in control of the future, despite your efforts?
2. Because Trevor Reynolds hadn't known a father's love growing up, he found it hard to trust in a loving God. Are you able to rest in the love of God, no matter what human relationships have done in your life?
3. Penny let angry words linger between herself and Brad, and then when he died, it was too late to ask for his forgiveness. Has anything similar ever happened to you? What did you learn about the importance of forgiving and being forgiven sooner rather than later?
4. Although he was young, Brad had a deep faith and the ability to love others. That

love drew others to him. Are you able to love those who are far from God, those whose personalities or lifestyles are different from your own?

5. The townsfolk of Kings Meadow pulled together to help a neighbor in need. God has given each of us a time and place to bond with and help others, and that begins with where we live. Have you found ways to reach out to your neighbors? In what ways do you care for those in need?

6. Trevor pursued a dream of fame as a singer that was never realized, despite his talent. What do you think about the lesson he learned from the book of Joshua regarding true success? Are you able to "offer up" the talent God has given you, for Him to use as He chooses rather than as you choose?

7. Do you have a favorite character from *Keeper of the Stars*? Who is it, and why?

ABOUT THE AUTHOR

Robin Lee Hatcher is the bestselling author of over seventy-five books. Her well-drawn characters and heartwarming stories of faith, courage, and love have earned her both critical acclaim and the devotion of readers. Her numerous awards include the Christy Award for Excellence in Christian Fiction, the RITA Award for Best Inspirational Romance, *Romantic Times'* Career Achievement Awards for Americana Romance and for Inspirational Fiction, the Carol Award, the 2011 Idahope Writer of the Year, and Lifetime Achievement Awards from both Romance Writers of America (2001) and American Christian Fiction Writers (2014). *Library Journal* named *Catching Katie* one of the Best Books of 2004.

Robin began her writing career in the general market, writing mass-market romances for Leisure Books, HarperPaperbacks, Avon Books, and Silhouette. In 1997, after several years of heart preparation, Robin accepted God's call to write stories of faith and hasn't looked back since. She has written both contemporary and historical women's faith-based fiction and romance for Thomas Nelson, Zondervan, Revell, Steeple Hill, Tyndale House, Multnomah, and WaterBrook.

Robin enjoys being with her family, spending time in the beautiful Idaho outdoors, reading books that make her cry, and watching romantic movies. Robin and her husband make their home on the outskirts of Boise, sharing it with Poppet, the high-maintenance papillon, and Princess Pinky, the DC (demon cat).